BAD GUY

LIA
STENNIS

BAD GUY

Lia Stennis

This book is dedicated to
Raya Stennis

PROLOGUE

KENDALL

My heart races as Natalie turns the knob on the safe. It's pounding so loud, I'm afraid it might wake my family upstairs. I try to calm myself down by reciting the numbers of the safe in my head as Natalie puts them in: Turn it to the right. 37. Turn it to the left. Pass it once. 13. Turn it to the right one more time. 42. Natalie turns the handle, and the safe opens up. Inside are two folders, and she takes both out. She hands them to me and notices my expression. She gives me a reassuring smile.

"Don't worry," she whispers, so quietly it's barely audible. "This is going to work." I try to smile back, but the knot in my stomach won't go away.

Natalie closes the safe as quietly as possible, and we begin to walk out through the kitchen and toward the back door. When we reach the door, Natalie hesitates for a moment. Once we walk through this door, we will be leaving this place, this family. For good. But the moment passes as quickly as it came, and as Natalie reaches for the handle, I try to get my head back in the game. Natalie slides the door open, and suddenly a deafening siren begins to blare.

I gasp and stop dead in my tracks. My blood runs cold. I frantically lock eyes with Natalie and see that she, too, looks panicked and just as uncertain as me. The noise must have been triggered by the door opening. It feels like it's coming from all around us.

Surrounding us. There's no point in trying to disarm something I can't locate. It's too late anyway.

I hear footsteps coming from upstairs.

My heart skips a beat, and I again find myself looking to Natalie for guidance. She'll know what to do. She always knows what to do.

"Run," she whispers.

No longer making any attempt to be quiet, we run out the door and across our backyard. Our house is surrounded by a thick forest that may as well be a jungle, and we run into the underbrush. Branches and thorns scrape my arms and legs, but I barely feel them. I follow Natalie blindly through the woods, not even knowing where she's leading us. All I know is that we have to run.

Suddenly, I hear a familiar voice call out, and I freeze. Sir. I turn and see three figures emerging from the house. I can only guess that the three figures are Ma'am, Sir, and one of my siblings. I hear Sir shout our names.

"Get down!" I hear Natalie whisper from behind me, and I feel her arm on my back pulling me to the ground. I drop down, so that my stomach is touching the forest floor, and look in the direction of the three figures. In the shadow of the moonlight, I see Ma'am and Sir with guns in their hands. I can almost feel my heart sinking. They must have found the plans missing in the safe. They're going to kill us. And I know that they will trek through these woods, turn every stone, clear through every bush, until they find us with those plans.

Just as I'm reaching this conclusion, Natalie gets up and tugs on my arm. She pushes me in front of her, putting herself between me and the house. I begin to run again, and I hear Natalie's footsteps following me. That's when I hear the loud *crack!* of a branch. I don't know which one of us made the noise, but it doesn't matter. Because Ma'am and Sir heard it, and that's when the gunfire starts. I hear bullets whiz past me, but I don't stop.

Soon enough we'll be out of range. We just have to make it a couple more yards. Just a couple more yards.

But of course, with our luck, we don't. I hear Natalie drop first, then I look behind me and see her lying in a pool of blood that is slowly forming, struggling to get up. The sight of her in pain makes me sick, but I force myself to run back for her. I see that she has been shot in her left leg, and I'm momentarily relieved. A leg shot can be treated. A leg shot won't kill her instantly.

I kneel down and throw her left arm over my shoulders. It isn't easy getting her up, especially since she's eighteen and five years older than me, but I use all the strength I have to lift her up onto her good leg. Once she is steady, we begin to slowly shuffle away from the house. She's dragging her bad leg behind her, and our pace is comparable to a slow walk.

"We're almost out of range," I say, as if trying to encourage her. "We're almost there." However, we're only a few yards out of range when Natalie collapses completely. I prop her up behind a tree, so that if any other bullets come our way, the tree will catch them first. The gunfire from Ma'am and Sir continues, which momentarily relieves me. If they're still shooting, it means that they don't know Natalie has been hit. That gives us time. But I realize that time won't help us now. I notice two more bullet wounds in Natalie's stomach, and my throat constricts.

"Oh my god." I hear my voice crack, and even to me, I sound pathetic.

The nearest road is another half a mile away from the house, and even if we made it, what then? Even if we were lucky enough to get a ride, they would have to take us to a hospital, where our identities could be exposed. We would be thrown in jail.

Natalie seems to be thinking the same thing as me, because she touches the side of my face with her right hand and says, "You have to go."

The full force of her words hits me like a truck, and I immediately want to unhear them.

"No," I say. I feel tears streaming down my face, and my voice trembles like I'm a scared little kid. "No!" I say it louder this time, as if my volume could drown out everything else in the world right now.

Natalie nods slowly. "Kendall, I'm not going to make it." She nods to her stomach wounds. Her voice is tight, like when she has a bad cold. I know she's trying to hide her fear, the way she always has for me. "The only way you will survive is if you leave me. You and I both know that."

"No!" I say, even louder this time. I feel like I'm actually being suffocated. This can't be happening. I can't lose Natalie. I can't. "No! No! I'm not leaving you! I won't leave you behind!" I try to form a plan in my head for how I could possibly get us both out of this situation alive, but nothing comes to me. Natalie puts her hands on either side of my face, locking her eyes with mine. That's when I realize I'm shaking. A small whimper escapes me.

"Kendall," Natalie says, her voice now strong and determined. "I need you to listen to me." All I can do is nod. "You cannot let them win. You can't let them have both of us." I know by "them" she means Ma'am and Sir. She slides her right hand down to the two files I'm clutching close to my chest. I had almost forgotten I had them. "You have to take those and get them as far away from here as you can."

I begin to shake my head.

"Nat…" I begin, my voice so weak it's practically a whisper. She shushes me before I can say anything more. She puts her hands back on the sides of my face and kisses the top of my head softly, like she used to do when I was little. Then she presses her forehead against my own.

"I love you," she says, her own voice trembling now. "More than anything in the world." She pauses and pulls away. We make eye contact, and her gaze is determined and unwavering. She has always been so brave. "And that's why you have to go." She pushes me away, and this time I don't resist. I look one last time at the only person I have ever loved, before I turn and run.

TWO YEARS LATER

CHAPTER ONE

KENDALL

I stand two blocks away. Hiding in an alley. My breathing is rapid, as it always is when I'm in the middle of an assignment. No. Not an assignment. A job. Assignments are a thing of the past. I don't *have* to do this. I *want* to do this. I hear a scratching sound behind me and turn to see my dog, Milo, pawing at a dead mouse. His claws make a scraping sound on the concrete, like a fork scraping the surface of a plate.

"Hey!" I whisper in a scolding tone. I grab his leash and kick the mouse to the back of the alley. He pulls a little but doesn't try too hard to get to the mouse, since he knows I disapprove. I drop his leash again, knowing he will not stray far from me. I'm the one that saved him, after all. Lost things like us know when to stay with a decent person.

I look back across the street. Alejandro is standing outside the bar, swaying slightly. He's clutching a beer bottle in his gloved hand. Of course, he's not actually drinking. Drinking on the job would be quite irresponsible. I filled that bottle with water this morning, so even the occasional sips he takes will not intoxicate him. After about two minutes, he removes his baseball cap with the hand he is holding the beer in, and without looking at me, he swipes his hand over his hair, as if wiping away sweat. This is my signal. I begin jogging, my dog at my side. The cord from my phone to my earbuds swings back and forth as I run, and my high ponytail follows suit. I finally had a growth spurt in these past couple years, so I almost look my age. My skin has tanned from the pale color that I developed all those years ago, and my hair has thickened into full, dirty blonde locks.

I maintain my pace, since there's really no hurry, and calling attention to myself by quickening my pace is the last thing I want to do. It takes me only a few minutes to reach the van, and even there I don't stop. Surprise, idiots! My phone doubles as a lighter. In one swift motion, I press the volume button, which causes a tiny lip of fire to come out of where the flashlight would shine. It is just enough to light the barely visible wick running along the side of the van. The main thing that worries me is that the fuse is purposely slow burning, so it will be visibly lit for about ten seconds before it reaches the inside of the van, where it will continue to burn.

My heart races. I always forget what this part of a job feels like. I could swear that the police will come around the corner and shoot me dead on the spot at any moment. I only have fifteen seconds to turn the corner and get as far as I can while still going at about the same pace, so as to not draw attention to myself. However, I feel myself quickening my pace as I turn the corner. I am counting the seconds in my head. Eight seconds left. There is a whole building between me and the van, I remind myself. I force myself to keep my pace, and Milo trots beside me. I know he has devices in his ears to save his hearing, but those won't save him if he is crushed by a piece of rubble. The same goes for me—my earbuds are supposed to dilute the sounds; however, Eduardo has reminded me time and time again that it will still be very loud. Three. Two. One. Boom.

CHAPTER TWO

DANIELLE

I look out the window to see the sky streaked with orange and pink. I know it must be about five o'clock at night, but I don't check my phone to confirm. My husband and I have this tradition of opening all our presents on Christmas Eve. I had never done this before I met him, but our first Christmas together, we decided to go hiking on Christmas day since it was in the mid-fifties and sunny that year. From then on, it became a sort of tradition. Tomorrow, we had pretty much nothing to do. We would probably watch some new Netflix series, or play with Layla, our rescue Pitbull. People tend to assume that since Jason and I are both in the police force and Layla is a Pitbull that she is in the K-9 unit. Of course, she isn't. She would never be any good at it. She loves people, despite her abusive past, and is a total cuddle bug. Jason and I never even bothered to look into getting her trained, since the worst she could possibly do is lick the criminals to death. We got her another one of those squeaky tennis balls that she loves so much for Christmas. I wish I was able to enjoy today. Christmas Eve, the presents, the time with my family, all of it. If only I'd never driven on Highway 465 that night on October 14. Then maybe I would be able to enjoy this Christmas without guilt or the gut-wrenching anger that I've carried with me every day since then. Then maybe I'd be happy right now.

"Dani," Jason calls, pulling me back to reality. He is holding his phone. "The station just called; they want us there immediately."

"But we're on vacation," I say, confused. "Tell them that."

He shrugs. "I already did. They said it's urgent. I think there was an explosion in Nashville." My jaw drops.

"How big?" I ask, already running through possible scenarios and how I would begin to unravel each one. Sometimes, I wonder if I think too much like a detective.

"I don't know," he responds. "That's all the information they gave me."

"Well then, let's go," I say.

~

What a mess, I think to myself. It was supposed to be my day off. Christmas Eve. I was supposed to be at home with Jason, opening the gifts we had gotten each other. But at least this will distract me from trying to enjoy my Christmas celebration.

When I get to the scene, I am among the first there, since I live so close to the city. From what I've been told, the explosion was caused by a gray van parked in the approximate location outlined in white tape by the few cops that arrived before Jason and me. The crime scene leader instructs me to collect forensic evidence to be examined later by our team. I'm a detective by profession, but I trained in forensics, and I was a forensic specialist before I got promoted. I grab my supplies and slide on a pair of yellow plastic gloves. I duck under the caution tape and immediately notice the widespread debris around where the van was parked. Engine explosions caused by coolant leaks or lack of oil mainly cause the front half of the car to explode and don't have nearly the blast radius of this one. For a van this size, an accidental engine explosion is unlikely.

I spot a small streak of white on the ground. I take an evidence bag from my pocket and bend down to pick it up. It is a small piece of what looks like hard plastic, with the edges charred black. I look around the crime scene and see no objects close to the explosion matching this color. I drop the small piece of plastic into the evidence bag so that our forensic scientists can examine it, but from my years on the force, I can make an educated guess as to what it is: a piece of PVC pipe, used to make homemade pipe bombs. This explosion was no accident. Someone blew up that van on purpose. And I have a long few days ahead of me.

CHAPTER THREE

_____

KENDALL

The van is a constant rumble under me. We will be driving a lot these next couple of days. The explosion was a distraction. Police from all over the country will be focusing on something like that. They're all teed up for exactly what we're about to hit them with.

"Chug, chug, chug, chug!" the gang chants around me. Juan, the only person besides Alejandro here whose name I know, is currently downing an entire keg of beer through a rubber straw. I've tried the stuff. Don't care much for it. There are about a dozen people in the van, including myself and Juan. The gang consists of all men, excluding myself, mainly Mexicans that Alejandro has known for a while. I only know Juan by name, but I recognize a few others—there's a man with one brown eye and one blue eye, and another with a long scar running from his left temple to the left side of his jawline. Apparently, they were all friends as teenagers who were able to make it across the border together. I have no birth certificate, and the gang is a group of illegal immigrants. This means that thus far, the U.S. government has no record of us. This significantly lowers the odds of us getting caught.

I only knew the gang by reputation before I met them, and Juan was the first I encountered. They are the largest crime unit in the state, yet they lack any sort of professionalism. They're good at what they do and half decent at covering their tracks—good enough to have avoided getting caught thus far, anyway. They're not the ideal group, but I trust Alejandro's leadership, and time to find a better one isn't a luxury I can afford. Still, I wish they would stop behaving like such idiots on a job. Especially Juan. Despite leading me to Alejandro, he has proven himself utterly useless. And with all that he's drinking, he'll be too hungover *next week* to help us with anything. Not to mention we'll be sleeping in this van until we have to go back to Tennessee. I leap to my feet and open the small window between the back of the van and where the driver and passenger seats are. I squeeze through it and plop down into the passenger seat next to Alejandro.

"Your gang members all seem very..." I glance in the rearview mirror to see Juan puking all over the back of the van. "Useful." I close the window so the stench of vomit isn't tempted to waft up here.

Even though Alejandro's eyes are trained on the road, I can feel his glare.

"Once we get there, they will be," Alejandro says. "Trust me, it will be like they're different people."

I arch an eyebrow at him before remembering he isn't going to look at me.

"If you say so."

"Oh, I do," he says. "Good job on the plan, by the way, kid. This is going to be the biggest stunt my gang has ever pulled off. After this, the whole world will know about us." He grins with his yellow teeth. I don't smile back.

"Congratulate me when it's done," I say flatly. "And when your gang gets themselves together. We only have eleven people on this job; everyone has to do their part."

That wipes the smile clean off his face.

"Don't worry, kid. After tonight, I'll throw out all the alcohol. That should give them enough time to sober up before our big day."

"I hope you're right," I say.

~

That night is supposed to be a celebration of the success of the first part of our plan. We stop in the middle of nowhere, pull into an empty field and turn the car radio on to listen to the news of our bombing. The gang members all get out of the car and begin drinking and dancing and being insanely loud. I stand against the side of the van, keeping watch. I'm glad Milo is back home with Cecelia. He doesn't like it when people yell. We think he was abused.

Cecelia is Alejandro's girlfriend. They've been together since before I first met and moved in with them about a year ago. Alejandro, Cecelia, and Eduardo. I'd only heard about them from the news and other sources, and I knew I needed manpower to pull this off. That was when I tracked down Juan. It was about a year and a half ago.

I had watched him exit the bar and begin to walk toward his car.

"Excuse me, sir," I had said. He turned to look at me, then shook his head and looked away. I cleared my throat and spoke again with as much authority as I could muster as a fourteen-year-old girl. "Excuse me, sir." He looked around, seeing if I could be talking to anyone else. When it became apparent that there was no one else in the lot, he turned to stare at me in confusion.

"Get lost, you little shit," he finally said, attempting to walk away once more.

"Juan Hernandez!" I said loudly, getting frustrated with him. Out of all the people in the gang, I had to track down this incompetent asshole. This time, he turned to look at me.

"How do you know who I am?" he asked accusingly.

"Sorry," I said. "I guess you don't want me yelling out your identity, but you're an uncooperative dick. Now, do you want to help me, or do you want to just stand there like an idiot?"

"How do you know who I am?" he repeated, his voice quavering with emotion. He took a menacing step closer to me. I mimicked his action and took a step toward him myself in order to assert my dominance and show him I was not afraid of him.

"Your last job," I replied. "A drug deal went wrong, the police busted you, and they got the whole thing on their body cam footage. Your gang all made it out alive. Impressive, yet you yourself were sloppy. It didn't take much for me to piece together the clues of your whereabouts."

"Are you like a miniature FBI agent or what?" he asked.

"I work alone," I said. "Now, here's what's going to happen. You're going to take me to your boss's house immediately."

"Or what?" he asked. "Are you gonna tell Mommy?"

"*Or* I leave an anonymous tip at the police station stating your involvement in several of the crimes associated with the Nashville Gang," I said. "The choice is yours."

"Wait...wha—" Juan stuttered. "Are you threatening me?" As if that wasn't *so* painfully obvious.

"*Yes*," I said condescendingly. His face contorted into a scowl.

"Just get into the goddamn car, you little bitch," he grumbled. I smiled. It was only after we had begun the drive to Alejandro's that I realized we were being tailed by a familiar face. However, instead of informing Juan, I decided to use it to my advantage. After driving through about a half hour of forest, we arrived at a cabin. When we stopped the car, a man ran out.

"Juan!" he exclaimed. "What is it? You know you are not to come to my home unless there is an emergency." Juan stepped out of the car.

"Yeah, yeah," he said. "Some kindergartener wants to talk to you. Says she has a business proposition or some shit." I got out of the car, and the man's brows knitted together in confusion.

"What's your name?" I asked, examining the man. He was about average build, with dark hair and tan skin. He appeared to be in his late thirties, but his face looked worn, making him look much older.

"Alejandro," he said. "Who the hell are you?"

"Kendall," I said. "And you have a man coming here to kill you."

"What?" Alejandro said loudly, as if he were an old man who could not hear me.

"A man was tailing our car," I said. "He is only a few minutes behind us. He is Caucasian, tall, broadly built; he barely fits in the seat. The only reason I know he is here to kill you is because I know who he is: Thomas Reid. Number one hitman to Victor Sanders. Head of the Sanders Gang. I imagine you have had some issues with them, with you being in the same general area. I imagine there is some competition between the two of you."

Alejandro seemed brighter than Juan and was piecing together what I was saying.

"How do you know Reid?" he asked.

"A business meeting back in the day," I said, trying not to give him any specifics. "And believe me when I say that when the Sanders Gang makes you an enemy, they take care of things very swiftly and efficiently." I sensed a twinge of fear creeping into Alejandro's expression. I smiled. "However, I have a proposition for you."

"And what's that?" Alejandro said, crossing his arms.

"I take care of him for you," I said, pulling up the right side of my t-shirt to reveal my gun holster. Alejandro was visibly taken aback by this but seemed to realize that I wasn't there as a hostile.

"So you're just going to take care of it?" he asked, seeming to be amused with my proposition. "Just to be nice? As a favor? I don't buy it. What's in it for you?"

"I want in," I said plainly. "I have a job for you and your gang. One that could make the Nashville Gang more infamous than the Mors Clan." At the mention of the Mors Clan, Alejandro's eyes widened. No one spoke of the Mors Clan. The Mors Clan was a predator, and a vicious one at that. In the areas they controlled, no one so much as mentioned them, as if reluctant to even acknowledge their existence. No one talks about the boogeyman like it's real. That ignites a flame. And the Mors Clan was very good at snuffing out flames.

Alejandro paused for a moment before the sound of an engine became apparent. He made eye contact with me and gave me a stern nod. So I took care of it, and we have been planning this job ever since.

Eduardo is already in Kentucky. He forged himself some fake credentials and already has a position in the spot we are planning on breaking into. Eduardo is good at forging stuff on computers, and really anything to do with technology. The three of us, we could do it all. With Eduardo's tech genius, Alejandro's leadership, and my planning down to the minute, we could run this thing all on our own. However, we are planning on breaking into Fort Knox.

Fort Knox.

Just the name of it makes my heart skip a beat. It's where the U.S. government keeps its main stash of gold, and it's known as one of the most heavily guarded places in the world. But ever since Eduardo hacked its security cameras, it has seemed less and less so. Our plan is flawless. There is almost no way that I can see it going wrong.

I see Juan run over next to me and barf yet again. I take a step away from him and groan in disgust. I mutter some profanities about him under my breath. I walk over to the other side of the truck and look for any signs of movement. Of course, there is no one. Suddenly, I catch movement out of the corner of my eye. I jump and take a step back, ready to break for the gun in the driver's seat.

"Hey, puta," says a familiar, scratchy voice. Juan. I recognize the word—Eduardo will say it every now and then when Milo gets annoying. It means bitch.

"Shouldn't you be getting drunk?" I shoot back.

"I think I've had my share of drinking for the night," he says. I arch my eyebrow at him, unconvinced.

"All the liquor's gone," he admits sheepishly.

I nod and look back out into the distance. I can feel Juan's eyes on me. I try to distract myself by keeping an eye out for anyone coming, but after a few minutes I can't take it anymore.

"OK, what is it?!" I burst out.

"Nothing," he says. "I just noticed you don't smile too much."

"Don't have much to smile about," I retort. I turn to him, suddenly feeling very uncomfortable. "Look, if you're just gonna keep staring at me all night, make yourself useful. Go inside and clean my gun for tomorrow."

He looks at me for a few more moments before heading into the van and doing as I said. I look over my shoulder and see the man with the scar on his cheek tripping repeatedly in an attempt to make it back to the van. Yeah, it's gonna be a long night.

CHAPTER FOUR

DANIELLE

My partner, Nicki James, walks into the room. It's December 26, and the first official day we're working on the case together, although I spent most of Christmas Day canvassing the scene and interviewing witnesses. Jason wouldn't stop grumbling about it, but it came as a relief to me, as I was able to get through Christmas as if it were any other work day.

"OK, I've interviewed everyone at the crime scene, and I have great news," Nicki says.

I turn from the reports I'm typing up on my desk. "What is it?"

"A couple people were having a photoshoot in the area. They were trying to shed some light on the need for renovations in the poorer areas of downtown," she says. "Their last picture was taken only a few seconds before the bomb went off." She hands me the file with her notes and the main photographer's address. I gape at her.

"Oh my gosh, Nicki," I begin. "This is..."

"Beyond lucky," she finishes.

"Yeah," I say in disbelief. How much luckier could you get? "Thanks, Nicki."

"No problem," she says. "Let's head over there and get the pictures."

As we get in the squad car I put in the directions for the address on the file. It's about a half hour drive from the station. Once we finally get there, we hop out of the car. The house is average sized; I'd guess that the photographer is a middle-class woman.

"OK, so the photographer's name is Jessica Owens," Nicki says, reading from the file. "She got married five years ago and has a two-year-old son."

"Great," I say. I walk up to the small front porch and knock on the door. I hear footsteps, and a tall man with ginger hair opens the door. He's a skinnier build but looks about six foot tall. "Hi, I'm looking for Jessica Owens. Is she here?"

"Yeah, she's my wife," he says, unsure. "Is she in some kind of trouble?"

"No trouble," Nicki says. "We just think she may have witnessed something."

He nods and turns away from us. "Hey, Jessica? There are some officers here who would like to talk to you!"

A woman with dark skin, and dark hair pulled up in a bun rushes down the stairs with a young child on her hip. The kid must be her son. She is short, no taller than five feet.

"Hello," I say. "I'm Detective Toole, and this is my partner, Detective James. May we come in?"

"Of course," she says, opening the door a bit wider so that we can come in. The house is a modern rustic style, with lots of pictures from around the world, mainly with people in them. One shows a group of young men and women on the beach while a homeless man sits on the boardwalk with a jar labeled "money." The contrast between the two is jarring yet seemingly purposeful. I recognize that she's trying to show the difference between the upper and lower classes. Interesting.

Jessica closes the door.

"Could you take him upstairs?" she says to her husband, handing him her young son. Her husband nods, and she gestures for us to follow her into the kitchen. "Can I get you anything, detectives?" she asks politely.

"No, but thank you," I say, glancing at Nicki.

"We received some information that you were there just before the bomb went off in Nashville yesterday," Nicki says.

"That's right," she says. "I was doing a photoshoot with a fellow photographer."

"Yes, she told us you left the scene a few minutes before the bomb went off, and she took some pictures after you left, including one taken only seconds before the bomb went off," Nicki says. "She says all the photos were uploaded to your computer. We would simply like to see them."

"Of course," Jessica says. "I can download them all right now."

"That would be great," I say.

Jessica walks over to a black bag hanging on a coat rack by the front door. She pulls out a gray laptop and walks back over to us. She opens it and pulls up some photos of the crime scene, as well as some others of downtown Nashville. She walks over to a drawer in the kitchen and pulls out a USB flash drive. She sticks it in the laptop and selects all the photos with yesterday's date on them. She clicks download, and within a minute all the images are downloaded. She hands me the flash drive.

"Thank you," I say. "And just for the investigation, did you notice anything unusual when you were taking photos?"

"Not really; it was just a regular cityscape shoot," she says, looking off into the distance as if trying to remember something. "Although..." She trails off.

"Although?" Nicki asks.

Jessica begins clicking through the photos. "I saw the location of the explosion on the news," she says, continuing to click through photos. "It was this one, right?" She stops and points to an image of a gray van at the site of the explosion.

"Yes," I say. The image of the van seems to spark her memory.

"I saw a man inside the van," she says. "About an hour before the explosion, I spoke to a man. He seemed to be better off than the majority of the people in town, so I asked if I could photo-graph him."

"What did he say?" I ask.

"He immediately said no," she says, then pauses in thought. "But…yes, I'm almost sure he was walking away from the gray van, as if he had just gotten out of it." Nicki scribbles vigorously on her notepad.

"You're sure of this?" I ask. "That he was walking away from the van?" Jessica nods. "Did you happen to see where he was going?"

"He walked over to the park, around the corner," she says. "The only reason I thought it was strange at all was because he got into a van identical to the one that I saw him walking away from."

I make eye contact with Nicki, who raises an eyebrow in ques-tion. I give her a slight shrug. I have no idea what this could be suggesting, but it's the best lead we have.

"Is that all?" I ask.

"Yes," she says.

Nicki grabs a business card out of her pocket with both my and her work numbers on it.

"Please feel free to call us if you remember anything else."

~

A half hour later, we are back at the station. At my desk, Nicki leans over my shoulder as I put the USB into my computer.

"All right," I say. "Let's see what's on this." It only takes a few seconds to upload the images; there are over 100 photos on it. We'll have to examine each one closely.

Nicki looks at me. "This could take a while."

I sigh. "Most things in our line of work do."

We open the first picture, and it shows a graffitied building only a few blocks away from the scene. The time stamp is 3:43 p.m. That's a little over an hour before the bombing. There is no one in the picture, so we click to the next one. The next one is a slightly different angle of the same building. Again, no people, no van, nothing that could be tied to the crime scene. We go through about forty pictures before we find a picture that shows the crime scene. Upon seeing the van, I begin to understand my opponent a bit better. The time is 4:36 p.m., about half an hour before the bomb went off. The van was already in place. In fact, it was placed absolutely perfectly. No one would be able to see who was driving because the driver's side was facing the abandoned building; however, the blast would still hit the club across the street. I wonder if the van was intentionally placed. Whoever my opponent is, they are either highly intelligent or extraordinarily lucky. I click through a few more photos, and these give different angles of the abandoned building. It looks like Jessica and the other photographer took pictures of it for about twenty minutes. There are multiple pictures of people in the general area, as well as several pictures that include the van. However, there are only two pictures with a person and the van in the same shot, and they are both of the same person. It is a young girl; she looks about fourteen or fifteen years old. She has wavy, dirty blonde hair and is walking her dog. The pictures of her were taken only a few minutes before the bomb went off. One shot captures a profile of her face, and in the other her back is turned to the camera, and she is about to disappear into an alleyway. I mentally mark her as a possible witness and move on to the next picture.

The next image is around the corner of the abandoned building, and the van is out of sight. There are only three pictures of that angle, and the last one was taken at the time the bomb went off. I assume it was only a few seconds before it went off. The last one features another person, running away from the direction of the van. My heart skips a beat. This could be our guy. However, my heart sinks when I see that it is the same teenage girl that was in the other photos.

"Wait!" Nicki exclaims. "That's the same girl from the earlier pictures."

"Yeah, I know," I say flatly. "But there's no way she could have done this. I mean"—I click back to the pictures of the van and point to the screen—"just look at the placement of the van. It's perfect. You can't see who's driving it because the driver's side is facing the abandoned building, but it's close enough to the club that it would cause some damage to it and the people inside. No way some kid thought of that."

"So maybe it wasn't her idea," Nicki says. "Maybe she's just the one who lit the fuse. Maybe she didn't have a choice."

"And on her way to blow up a van, she brought her dog?" I say doubtfully.

Nicki sighs. "You're probably right."

Suddenly, a thought hits me. "Wait!" I exclaim. "I interviewed everyone at the crime scene!"

"Yeah, I know," Nicki says.

"There were no minors in the area. I didn't interview any. Did they identify the bodies at the scene?"

"I think so," Nicki says. She rushes over to her desk, which is right next to mine. She opens a file drawer and runs her fingers through the files until she finds the right one. She pulls the manila folder out of the drawer and runs back over to me. "The two bodies were identified as 42-year-old Brenda Woodward and 31-year-old James Dawn." Nicki looks up at me, an excited twinkle in her eyes. "So if she wasn't interviewed, and she wasn't among the deceased—"

"Maybe there is something to her," I finish.

CHAPTER FIVE

KENDALL

The time spent in the van was less than ideal. The smells of vomit, alcohol, and sweaty men all mixed together eventually found their way to my nose. It's been two days since the bombing in Nashville, and we are still on the road. The raid will take place tonight. I try to repress any feelings of anxiety, but they still manage to seep in. I've never pulled a job on my own. Granted, I'm not on my own—I have Alejandro, Eduardo, and a group of buffoons that don't seem to respect me—but this is the first job I've devised entirely on my own. I've thought about this a lot. The possibility of this all going south. My failure. What a fool I would make of myself if the gang got arrested at the gates. But we won't. We can't. With Eduardo on the inside, it would be hard for our plan to fail that soon. The worst possible outcome I can see is that we are killed on the inside, which if everything goes according to plan, shouldn't happen.

I open a bag of Doritos and bite into one. I relax a bit, letting the food calm my nerves. Comfort food, is what Natalie called it. I remember when we ate these for the first time. We couldn't stop laughing, because we had never tasted anything so good— *STOP*, I tell myself. I can't allow myself to become immersed in memories with Natalie. I have to stay focused, no matter what. If I let myself think about my past, it will only distract me, putting the lives of others and my own life at risk.

Alejandro stops the car, jerking me out of my thoughts. We're at the predesignated site for our operation to begin. I glance at Alejandro, and he gives me a nod. The two of us grab our gear and get out of the car. The gang gets ready in the back, and we step out front. My outfit consists of a pair of black leggings; a black zip-up sweatshirt made of the type of material used for work-out clothes, so the fewest stains cling to it; and over that a black bulletproof vest. I put an earpiece in my ear and slip on a pair of metallic black gloves. The last thing I need is for the authorities to get my fingerprints. We need to cover our tracks enough so that we don't get caught, but not far enough that the world won't know it was us. Just the right balance.

"Nervous?" Alejandro asks, eyeing me as he begins to gear up.

"No," I answer, hoping he won't inquire further.

"I just checked in with the gang," he says. "They're almost ready." I don't feel like commenting on the gang's inefficiency, so I just nod and look in the window of the van to check the time.

"Two minutes," I say. We can't stay for too long. The longer we sit here, the more cars will pass us, and the more people could ID us. But we need to give ourselves enough time. Five minutes seems like plenty.

"You remember the plan?" I ask Alejandro.

"You think I've forgotten it in the past twenty minutes?" he asks. I glare at him.

"I wouldn't put it past you," I retort, which coaxes a smile out of Alejandro. Suddenly, I hear the gentle droning of an engine. Squad 107. They're here. Alejandro makes eye contact with me.

"Right on time."

Attempting to get into Fort Knox as a visitor or even a government official is next to impossible. Just for a visitor to enter through the main doors, they must go through fourteen different full body scans, remove their clothing, and change into the uniform issued by the facility, on top of having a full background check beforehand. If you had ever been charged for so much as a DUI, you would be arrested for attempting to enter. When you are escorted through the halls, you are only walked through the areas with the most security cameras, surrounded by maximum security, nowhere near the gold or the weapons vault. Like I said, impossible. However, getting in as a guard working for Fort Knox, that was a possibility. Every few months, the guards on duty at Fort Knox are sent out of the facility, and a new shipment is sent in. Working at Fort Knox is rigorous and cannot be done for more than a few months at a time. The switching is random, however. Not even the guards themselves know when they will be switched out until the day of. But we were able to crack the code. We knew that the guards would be shipped in even before they did. Of course, not all of the guards are sent out, only the ones guarding the perimeter. There is only a fifteen-minute window between when the guards leave and when the new shipment is put into position. This is more than enough time for us to take action.

The military van comes into view, and Alejandro frantically waves his arms. I take a breath and push any thoughts that could distract me out of my mind. I can't afford for this to go wrong. I clear my head and focus on the van that is coming into my view.

The van stops on the road but doesn't pull over. There are two men in the front seat, both dressed in military uniform from head to toe. I know that there are about a dozen other soldiers in the back of the van.

"Excuse me, I'm sorry to bother you," Alejandro says politely. I walk over next to him. "Our car just broke down, and if you wouldn't mind—" His next words are cut off by gunshots as I shoot both men in the head. Both quick and clean kills. A commotion ensues in the next few seconds, and the new recruits in the back begin to open the back doors of the van to attack us. Alejandro pounds his fist against the side of our van twice. Taking the signal, the gang jumps out of the van and immediately gains the element of surprise over the soldiers running out of the military vehicle. One by one, the unarmed soldiers are shot down by the gang.

For a moment, silence rings in the air as we process what just happened. I am the first to move.

"OK, people! Let's hurry it up! We're on a time crunch here!" I yell, snapping the gang into action. The soldiers were all shot execution style, just like we had planned, so the blood on their uniforms is minimal. We won't need them for long, but we will need them long enough to get onto the grounds. If the security officers suspect something, they will lock down the facility, and the plan will be ruined. Luckily, there are more dead soldiers than gang members who need uniforms, so we have our pick of the litter. The majority of the gang quickly begins to remove the uniforms from the soldiers, Alejandro and Juan get the first pick since they will be sitting in the front seat, while two members of the gang start to load the bodies and weapons into the back of our van. Their job is to dispose of the van, cut a hole in the electric fence, which Eduardo should be disabling once we get inside, and get to the rendezvous point, where there should be another car waiting for us that Eduardo was supposed to have set up this morning. I quickly put an earpiece in my ear that I will use to contact Alejandro and Eduardo once we're in. I get in the back of the van with the rest of the gang following me in. I knew I wouldn't be able to pass as a soldier, so while the rest of the gang is tasked to get us in, I'll be our muscle once we are.

I holster my gun, not wanting to risk shooting any of the gang members once we are in the military van. Alejandro and Juan take the front seat, while I let the gang sit between myself and the back doors of the van. The doors close, and I feel the rumble of the engine as we start to move. We drive for about five minutes in absolute silence before we stop. I can feel my heart in my throat as I hear an unfamiliar voice.

"Squad number and code?" the voice asks.

"Squad number one-oh-seven," Alejandro replies. "Washington, fifteen." There is a deafening moment of silence between us. I know that is the right code for this unit—everyone has a different code, but it wasn't nearly as hard to decipher as one might think. But if Alejandro had said the wrong one...*buzz!*

I hear the gates open, and the car begins to move forward once more. I let myself relax momentarily. We're on the grounds now. Alejandro continues to drive forward until he is stopped once again, no doubt at the entrance to the Fort. The car comes to a stop, and the engine completely turns off. I hear the driver and the passenger door open just as another voice speaks.

"Who are you?" the guard asks.

"New squad," Alejandro says. "One-oh-seven."

"Alright, just let me make sure you're on the—" The voice is stopped by a loud *bang!* I hear a scuffle, no doubt between Alejandro, Juan, and the second guard, which eventually stops. There's no way to tell who won. Juan throws the doors to the back of the van open, and for once in my life I smile when I see him. He motions for the gang to get out, and they obey, leaving me inside. He returns with Alejandro and two more members. They carry the bodies of the two guards between them and dump them in the back of the van. They close the doors, and I am plunged into darkness. I hear the distinct sound of a garage door opening, only louder and heavier, as if it were a garage built to house a tank, which I suppose it is. I hear muffled voices outside the car, until finally I hear the front door open and close, alerting me that someone is in the driver's seat. It's standard procedure when new squads come on the grounds for their van to be housed in the garage and inspected while the squad themselves are searched for weapons before being supplied with the government-issued ones, which is why the gang didn't bring any of the weapons used to kill Squad 107.

The van begins to move forward, and I squat down behind one of the seats, taking my gun out of its holster. I hear the garage door close and get ready to pounce. The doors open, and light comes streaming in. My eyes hardly have time to adjust before a lone soldier sees the bodies of his incapacitated colleagues in the van. He stumbles backward.

"What the—" he exclaims, before I jump out of the shadows and fire two shots. He drops instantly. Another person yells something else that I can't quite make out. Nevertheless, I take it as a sign that he is coming my way and leap out of the van. Out of the corner of my eye, I see the gang being led out of the room, but I can't worry about them now. I see the second man running toward the body of the first soldier. When he sees me, he reaches for the pistol in the holster of his belt, but he's too slow. I shoot him dead. I scan the room quickly, making sure that there is no one else in the room, when suddenly, a deafening alarm goes off. I instinctively aim my gun in the direction the noise is coming from, only to realize it is out of bullets. I drop the gun next to the two bodies so it can't be traced back to me later and see Juan beating up the soldier that led them in. I run toward them.

"What the hell happened?" I exclaim.

"Our timing was wrong," Alejandro yells. "They inspected the truck before we had even left the room. He heard the commotion in here and sounded the alarm."

"Did you at least pass the search?" I ask. Alejandro nods and gestures around the corner. I know the blueprints of this place like the back of my hand, so I know he's gesturing to the weapons supply room.

"The gang and I will take the incoming guards," he says and puts an earpiece in his ear. "Go find Eduardo. He may need your protection." I know there's no time to argue, so I obey and run toward the biggest gold vault in America.

CHAPTER SIX

DANIELLE

I check my watch and groan. It's 5 in the afternoon. I was supposed to be home an hour ago. I pull out my phone and text Jason that it's gonna be a late night at the station. He should be used to it by now. I almost always stay past my hours when I'm on a case like this. The girl had been a dead end. I ran her face through every facial recognition system I could think of but came up with nothing. The kid has no previous record. When I told Nicki this, she said that the girl could have realized she dropped something or turned back for some reason and had gotten so close to the van that there would not have been a body for us to find. She is looking through missing children reports right now to see if anything comes up. However, in terms of suspects, we've hit a brick wall. The man who Jessica Owens identified didn't come up in any other witness reports or any of the photos. We called once to ask if she would be able to give a detailed enough description to a forensic artist. She could not.

I begin looking through my notes from when I questioned people at the crime scene. They all gave me their full name, address, and phone number so I could call them or go to their house if I needed more information. No one besides Owens had really given any information about a suspect or anything that pointed to one. I run through my memories of the questioning, and still, no one stands out in my mind. Everyone was very willing to comply, just a little rattled. I close my notebook and begin looking through the pictures again for anyone near the crime scene, even long before the bomb went off. But still, the only person who was close enough was that girl. I don't get it. There was no way she could have left the scene before the police got there, and yet her body wasn't at the scene either. It's as if she just vanished into thin air.

I open Google and look up how people's bodies respond to being so close to bombs. My mother was a doctor, and she always tells me that one of the many great things about being a doctor is that you never stop learning. Even in the operating room, there were times when she would look up different ways to treat something or different conditions that certain patients had. No shame in trying to learn more.

I click on a video that looks promising and somewhat professional. It begins with a middle-aged man with a beer belly introducing himself.

"I'm Joshua Forchus, and I work for the National Center of Defense for the United States," the man says in a voice that I could only describe as a teacher's. "Today we will be demonstrating how human bodies react to large explosions. The purpose of this demonstration is to emphasize the importance of maintaining a safe distance."

It shows a white dummy with no face or any distinctive features next to a black box about the size of a shoe box. The box is supposed to represent the explosive, and the layer of fabric on the dummy is about the thickness of human skin. It shows the bomb going off multiple times with the dummy ten yards farther away each time. The dummy gets more and more torn up as it gets closer to the explosion, but even when it's extremely close, there is still residue. Even if the girl had sprinted back toward the van in the few seconds before the bomb went off, I'd guess she would be twenty to forty yards away from the bomb. In that range, a human would undoubtedly be killed, but they would not be completely disintegrated. Even at twenty yards, there would be some residual body parts or at least enough human tissue to see that someone had been killed. I let out an exasperated sigh and close out of the video. Another dead end.

Suddenly, I hear a droning sound behind me. It's as if a hive of bees has suddenly awoken and is now buzzing about the station. I turn around and see the chief, as well as the couple dozen officers that are still here, all suddenly looking panicked. A few get up and run out of the office, and a couple of others immediately pick up their phones and call for backup.

I walk up to the CSI whose desk is closest to mine. He has dark brown hair and hazel eyes and stands at six foot six. His name is Darius. We are casual friends—he's been to my house for dinner a few times. He's intelligent, but what I truly admire about him is his prowess in the lab. He's by far the best CSI in our precinct, and his skills are definitely better than mine had been.

"Darius, what's going on?" He looks up at me.

"Dani, you won't believe it," he says in the calm voice with the subtle undercurrent of panic that he always uses when he's found something incriminating. "Someone broke into Fort Knox!"

CHAPTER SEVEN

KENDALL

"Hurry up!" I whisper-yell to Eduardo. His pad is hooked up to the control panel on the white wall. We are standing in front of a silver metal door that hides the largest supply of gold in the U.S. This is taking too long. Every cop in the country must be on their way here right now. We need to be moving faster.

"I'm doing my best!" Eduardo whispers back and continues to type random things into his pad. I hear footsteps coming down the hall and whip around. We've been taking too long. We're busted. I know it. A man in his early thirties dressed in a military uniform runs down the hall with a gun that I recognize as an AR-15. He has dark hair and eyes, and judging by his age, he has to be new here. His more experienced coworkers are likely busy with Alejandro and the rest of the gang. When he sees me, a look of astonishment, then confusion crosses his face, and he hesitates for a moment. Thankfully, a moment is all I need. My priority is the gun. I'm sure he has other weapons on him, but the AR-15 is the only imminent threat. I push down the weapon in its lowered position and hold it there, then I bring my knee up to the man's groin. As he doubles over, I can see him reaching for something else on his belt—a taser, I'd guess. I only let my foot lightly tap the ground before bringing my knee up a second time, this time making contact with the man's skull. As the man staggers back, he drops his gun and attempts to punch me. However, he must have gotten a concussion from the blow to his head, and his attempted hit is sloppy. I dodge it easily and grab the gun. His eyes go wide at the sight of my hands on the weapon, and he lunges for my legs. I don't have enough time to turn the gun and instead bring the butt down on his head. This time, the blow to his head knocks him unconscious, and he falls to the ground. He lies there on his stomach, and I can feel eyes on me. I turn to see Eduardo gaping at me. He's never seen me fight before.

"You better hurry up; there will be more of them coming!" I snap at him, annoyed. He nods and gets back to the pad. I crouch down and inspect the soldier's belt. The only weapons that are visible from the back are his taser and a knife. I check the taser, making sure the safety is on. Satisfied that it is, I shove it in my pocket. I grip the knife and feel its weight. I can see that the knife is purely for self-defense, as the sides are blunt and only the tip is sharp—that, I'm sure, is good for stabbing.

"I got it!" Eduardo exclaims, and just like that, the doors open, revealing more gold than I could have ever imagined existed in the world. Bars upon bars of gold just piled up in an orderly heap that is twice as tall as me. My jaw drops, and I almost laugh. The American government has this kind of wealth, and they allow their people to suffer and starve. They don't even do anything with this gold; they just keep it locked up and pour resources into keeping it that way. No matter. This will all be put to good use soon.

I put my hand to the earpiece in my ear.

"We're in," I say, alerting the gang.

I hear more footsteps coming down the hall. Damn it. I turn around and see two soldiers dressed identically to the one earlier. Unfortunately, they are also identically armed. However, like their predecessor, they see me and hesitate for a moment. Now armed, I take the opportunity to pull out my taser, and before the guard on the right can react, I pull the trigger, and he lets out a scream. The taser makes contact with his chest, and he falls to the ground. This gives the other soldier enough time to identify me as a threat, and he aims his gun toward me.

"Freeze!" he yells. I can feel Eduardo's eyes on me from behind, and I know he has no idea what to do. It would take less than a second to pull the trigger, but I have a good hunch he won't because I'm a kid. I can still walk away from this. My one tase is used up, but I still have the knife on me. An idea forms in my head. I slowly put up my hands and drop the taser.

"Do as he says," I instruct Eduardo. For a moment there is no response, but after a few seconds I hear him set his tablet on the ground and know that he must have followed my lead. Just as I predicted, once we both appear non-hostile, the guard takes one hand off the gun and puts it on the walkie-talkie strapped to his chest. He takes his eyes off us for a few seconds. Before he can get a word in, I grab the knife from my pocket with my right hand and move toward him, keeping my body out of his line of fire. With my left hand, I push the barrel of his gun down. With only one hand on the weapon, he doesn't have the strength to counter the motion. I raise my right hand, blade in hand, and slit his throat. The motion is swift, and the guard hardly has enough time to react. He makes a choking sound, and after a few seconds he falls to the ground. I stab him in the back of the neck, right where his spinal cord is, ensuring his death. I then grab the AR-15 off the ground where it fell out of his hands and move into the room full of gold.

Eduardo turns to me and gestures to the large pack on his back. I walk over to him and open it. We begin stuffing as many bars of gold into it as we can, and I hear footsteps behind me again. I grab the gun and point it at the door just as Juan walks in, a rifle slung around his chest. His eyes grow wide at the sight of me, and he puts his hands up.

"Don't shoot!" he yells. I lower the gun. He walks in the door, and Alejandro follows with the rest of the gang.

I glare at him, then holler to the rest of the gang, "Hurry up! We don't have much time." Everyone in the gang except for me has large backpacks, and we begin putting the gold bars in them. We are about halfway done when I hear another set of footsteps come down the hall. I turn to Juan and raise my eyebrows in question. Could there be another member of the gang coming? He shakes his head, and I raise the AR-15 rifle once more.

"Everybody keep doing what you're doing!" I yell. "I'll handle this!" The gang must already be exhausted from the fight on the way here. I can't risk our lives with their potentially sloppy fighting. Just as I move to the front of the doorway, the bullet hits me. It knocks the wind out of me, and I fall to the ground. However, it doesn't penetrate the bulletproof vest. I look at the soldier, and a look of shock registers on his face. He thinks he just killed a child. These soldiers are all wearing military grade armor on everything but their head and limbs. That's where I'll have to aim then. I quickly sit myself up, prop the rifle on my knee as a rest, and take aim with the gun. The optics are better quality than I've ever shot with, and I shoot the soldier in the head easily.

Suddenly, I hear an army of footsteps coming toward me. However, the door is only big enough for one person to get through at a time. A smart strategy for keeping people like us out, but not so smart when you're trying to get in and ambush us yourself. I don't move my crosshairs from where the first soldier entered and only have to move them up slightly when the first soldier enters. I pull the trigger, and the soldier that follows doesn't even have time to react to the first one going down before I kill him too. After the third one follows, the soldiers begin to catch on, and the next one doesn't walk in.

I stand up and back up from the door with my crosshairs still on the doorway. Still, no one walks in. I know they're out there...so what is their plan? I risk turning my head and see that there is considerably less gold than before but still much more left to put in packs. I'd like to clear out this room. I turn my head back to the door and see that no one is entering. What are they planning?

I hear a loud whirring sound behind me and see that the wall behind the gold is moving. It's peeling upward and folding in on itself like a garage door. It opens fully to reveal an army. There must be hundreds of soldiers behind that door, and they're waiting to corner us. Well, shit. Of course they wouldn't put everything in the damn blueprints. Our best escape route is the door we came from. There's no way we can get through that many soldiers. I get to my feet and poise my gun to shoot at a not-yet-visible enemy from the doorway we entered through.

"Everybody this way!" I yell. No one questions my decision before following me. Just as I suspected, the first soldier comes through the small door, and I shoot him on sight. We will be considerably slower on the way out with all the gold on our backs, but everyone is riding an adrenaline rush, so they should be able to keep up. I hear a chorus of gunshots behind me and am almost certain that my hearing will be permanently damaged after this. A few of the gang members are shooting as well, so the task of taking out the soldiers does not entirely fall to me. We move forward, taking out a dozen or so soldiers altogether.

By the time we get to the door, I realize that they must have been mainly relying on the soldiers coming from behind to take us out, because there are only another dozen or so soldiers in the hall when we step out. I notice that I took another bullet to my back, but I was mostly guarded by the members of the gang behind me. I'm sure I'll feel it later. The gunfire is almost instant, but I remind myself that they would need to shoot one of us in the head to kill us. They haven't figured that out yet, I guess.

I turn on my heel and run in the opposite direction of the soldiers to where I know the emergency exit is. I turn left and see five or so soldiers there. I know we're outgunned. I can't risk shooting at them because even if we did make it through, a few of the gang members might not. My best chance is hand-to-hand combat, which sounds like suicide right about now. However, I remind myself that like the other guards, they are not expecting a minor, so I have the element of surprise.

I walk up to them as if they are not even there, and they all hesitate at the sight of me. What a bunch of blithering idiots. I only have time to shoot one in the head before another marks me as a target. I turn my gun around and hit the one next to him in the head with the butt of my gun. This knocks him out cold, and the rest of the guards can't seem to decide between shooting me or aiming for the gang. One of them to my right punches me in the face, and for a moment the world blurs around me. I lift my head back up and snap back into focus.

"You're gonna regret that, buddy," I say. I put a hand on his shoulder and another on his head. I twist his jaw and pull. He falls to the ground, his neck broken. The guard standing next to him sees this and gapes. He attempts to turn his gun toward me, but the barrel is too long and I'm too close. The hot barrel only touches my left shoulder before I get my right arm over the gun and throw it out of his hands. I don't turn around before elbowing him in the throat. I whirl around and grab his right shoulder with one hand and his right elbow with the other, pulling him toward me as I bring my knee up to his solar plexus. This stuns his diaphragm, and he falls to the ground. The last one hits me in the stomach with the butt of a gun. I fall to the ground, trying to catch my breath.

As I lie there, gasping for air that doesn't seem to want to come into my lungs, I see the guard turn the gun on Eduardo. I manage to prop myself up slightly and kick the guard in the side of the knee. His knee buckles, and he loses his balance. I use this opportunity to sweep at the back of his other knee, which knocks him off his feet. He loses his grip on the gun and begins to fumble and swat for it. As he falls to the ground, I sit up a bit more and hit the gun out of the air before his hands can find it. It skids across the floor, away from him. It hits someone's foot, and I look up to see that it's Alejandro. He grabs it off the floor and shoots the soldier in the head. He walks over to me and holds out his hand to help me up. I take it, and he hoists me to my feet.

"Nice job, kid," he says.

"We have to go," Eduardo says, making for the door. He opens the emergency exit, which sets off a loud blaring noise. We make a break for the barbed wire fence. We run across the open field, which only stretches for a fraction of a mile before we reach the large electronic fence with barbed wire on top. Eduardo disabled the fence before we got in, and I don't hesitate to crawl through the hole that the rest of the gang made with bolt cutters. I go through first and wait for Eduardo, then Juan, and six other members of the gang to crawl through the opening. That means everyone made it out alive. Just as the last guy is about halfway through the fence, I hear yelling and footsteps running toward us. The second he makes it all the way through, an army of soldiers runs out onto the field. There must be at least sixty of them. Maybe more.

"Eduardo!" I yell, adrenaline pumping through my veins, ready to run.

"I'm working on it!" he says, getting his tablet out of his bag. He taps on it a few times before the electric fence hums to life. I smile as the first soldier attempts to make it through the hole and gets electrocuted on contact with the fence.

"Run!" I yell, and everyone obeys. The gunfire roars behind us. A bullet catches my arm, and another skims my leg. I know that my adrenaline must be through the roof, because I don't feel the pain yet, only the heat. More hit my bulletproof vest, but these only leave bruises. I wonder how much more the armor can take.

I hear a yelp behind me and know that someone must have been hit. We keep running along the main road until the gunfire behind us quiets down. I know we must be out of range. When a fork in the road comes, we have the option to go right, onto a backroad, or to the left and keep going onto the main road. We head right, knowing that every cop in the fucking country must be on their way here, and the only reason we aren't being chased right now is because we trapped the soldiers from Fort Knox in their own compound. We run for about half a mile on the dirt back road through the woods before we come upon a run-down neighborhood. The houses look like they are on the brink of collapse, and something tells me it wouldn't be too much of a stretch to say that most of them don't have people living in them.

At the entrance of the neighborhood are two of the gang members in a brand new white minivan. It also has a new license plate number that no one else in the state has, so it can't be traced back to anyone. He opens the door of the minivan, which is an automatic. We hop in, and he speeds down the street. The interior of the car is a sleek gray, and in this run-down neighborhood, we stick out like a sore thumb. I can feel my heart rate slowing a bit, and I begin to feel the full brunt of my wounds. I examine my right wrist where the first bullet hit me. It seems like it just grazed me. It's bleeding less than before but still quite a bit. I tear off a strip of my shirt and wrap it around the wound. Not the worst bullet I've ever taken. I wonder how long it will take to heal. The one in the back of my left calf is another matter. I know the bullet made more of an impact there, taking off a large chunk of skin. I grit my teeth as I try to move it. I'll have to treat it as soon as I get the chance. It's not bleeding much so I know that the only real danger is infection.

No one speaks for a long time until Eduardo breaks the silence.

"Hey, kid." It takes me a moment to realize he's talking to me. I'm still a little out of it, I guess, but the job did make me feel better. I turn to him but don't say anything.

"Where did you learn to fight like that?" he asks. Normally, I would avoid a real answer to that question, but the adrenaline must still be affecting my mind, because before I can think, I answer it.

"My mother was an assassin," I say quietly. "She taught me."

The rest of the ride is silent.

CHAPTER EIGHT

DANIELLE

The squad car comes to a screeching halt as we pull to the side of the road. Jason's driving, I'm in the passenger seat, and Nicki's in the back. I look at the large white building with a wire fence that is Fort Knox. Whenever Jason and I passed it on our road trips to Lake Michigan in the summer, it had always seemed so massive and secure. I had always perceived it as impossible to penetrate. Now, it seems so run down, so small. So humiliated. What kind of message is this sending to the people of America? That the government is weak? That we are not capable of protecting our own wealth? No telling. We just have to catch these people as soon as possible and make an example of them. Show the world that no one messes with the American government.

I get out of the car, and the cold air whips my face. When I see the dozens of police cars and helicopters surrounding the building, a wave of anger comes over me. Any one of these people could aid in the investigation. But no, it has to be me and Nicki. Even though we already have a huge case on our hands, we have to aid in the investigation of whoever broke into Fort Knox because the Nashville Police are short-staffed. We really need to get on that. So much for my Christmas vacation. It doesn't look like I'll be getting any time off anytime soon. The feds are already here, and I'm sure the FBI is as well. I can see some police trying to keep what must be a hundred journalists and reporters behind the yellow tape. I see a female reporter trying to push through the crowd of police officers to get a good view of the building. Another is shoving a microphone and camera in an officer's face. It looks like pure chaos over there. This will be the story of the century.

Nicki and Jason get out of the car, and I see Jason lock the doors. Good. No telling what a crowd this large will do unattended. We walk over to the entrance of Fort Knox, where most of the police cars are, and duck under the yellow tape. A man with a badge that reads *FBI* greets us.

"Hello," Jason says, extending his hand to the officer. "We're members of the Nashville City Police Department. We're here to help. If you don't mind me asking, what exactly happened here?"

The man takes Jason's hand and shakes it. "Good to have you," he says. "The short story is, a group of criminals broke into the facility and stole at least a few million dollars worth of gold. The rest of it is being transported to a secure location as we speak. The break-in was well planned out and well executed, which leaves us in a tight spot. We would like to make this go away as quickly as possible, and frankly, we don't quite have the manpower for it. That's why we need you. We apologize for bringing you all here on such short notice, but could you tell me all of your qualifications so I can put you to work?"

"Officer Toole has been on the force for seven years," I say. "Detective James and I are partners, although I do have training in forensics if that could be applied in any way."

The officer nods and gestures toward Nicki and me. "You two, go inside. Agent Danvers will assign you a task." He then gestures toward Jason. "You, with me. We need to keep this damn crowd in check." Jason and the officer walk away, and Nicki and I walk into Fort Knox.

On any other occasion, I would be ecstatic to enter the esteemed Fort Knox. The entrance is grand, made of marble and with the U.S. seal carved onto the floor in gold. It feels like a patriotic mansion housing an eccentric billionaire, not the largest supply of gold in the United States.

My attention is diverted to an officer in the middle of the room. She is pale, with short blonde hair and a name plate that reads *Danvers*. Nicki and I walk to her.

"Hello, I'm Federal Agent Danvers," she says in a surprisingly authoritative voice.

"Hello," I say. "I'm Detective Toole, and this is my partner Detective James." Agent Danvers gives us a nod.

"Thank you both for coming here on such short notice. We need everyone we can get on this case," Agent Danvers says.

"We understand," Nicki says. "How can we help? Detective Toole has forensics training, and I am willing to help in any way I can."

"I'm glad to hear that," Agent Danvers says, "because there is plenty for you two to do." She points to a hallway to her left. "Detective James, first door on the right is a room full of witnesses. There are already some people interviewing them, but I'll need you to assist them." Nicki nods and walks off into the hallway. "Detective Toole, please follow me." Agent Danvers turns around, and I follow her down a long white hallway to a room swarming with at least a dozen other detectives. Yellow cones stand directly in front of the door. The white outline of a body is marked on the floor in tape, and there's blood everywhere. I know that there used to be a body there. There is a gun on the floor, an AR-15 by the looks of it. I peer into the room, which is completely empty of anything other than detectives, their equipment, and hundreds of yellow cones. I realize what it is immediately.

"This is where they stole the gold from," I say.

"Yes, this was one of the many main storages for gold bars," Agent Danvers says. "This is where the intruders broke in and began their rampage. The inside is all taken care of; we need you to assist in the examination of the hallway." She gestures to the tape outline and the gun.

"There used to be a body here," I say, putting on my gloves. I squat down and begin reading the labels on the yellow cones. "How did they die?"

"Slit throat," Agent Danvers says. "Male officer."

I look up at her and gesture to the gun on the floor. "But he had a gun to protect himself. How could he have been killed by someone with a knife?"

"That's what we are trying to figure out," Agent Danvers says. "As a matter of fact, we are going through the security cameras right now. Now, I'll leave you to your work." I give her a nod, and she turns and walks away.

I begin to survey the crime scene. There is blood everywhere, and I begin to get an idea for who I'm dealing with here. Whoever this was had to be highly trained or had backup. To go up against a professional toting a semi-automatic with a knife and *win*, you'd really have to know your way around the weapon, to say the least.

I pick up the gun. There is a lot of blood on it, and it would be hard to get a solid print off of it. Not that I'd expect to get a print off of someone who robbed a government facility this big. If they're as professional as the officer in the front described, they would have some precautions to not leave behind evidence. I'm getting my print kit out of my bag when something catches my eye. Caught in the action of the gun are a couple strands of long dirty blonde hair. They almost blend in with the black gun and could be missed at first glance. We would have to get it DNA tested to figure out whose it was, but Danvers said the victim was a male, so this was likely from his killer. Even if he had long hair, which I'm sure wouldn't be allowed in the professional setting of Fort Knox, it would have to be tied up out of the way. Even so, something about the hair seems familiar. I pull out an evidence bag and tug the hairs out of the gun. I drop them in the bag and seal it. I'm only beginning to label it when I hear footsteps. I look up and see Nicki running up to me. I quickly finish the label then stand up.

"What is it?" I ask. My unease only grows as I register Nicki's panicked expression.

"Dani, the soldiers, they said it was a kid," she says. "A kid attacked them. A little girl." At first, I'm confused. A little girl came to Fort Knox and attacked the guards? Then I realize why the hair looked familiar. I've seen it before. Yesterday. In the pictures taken in Nashville on Christmas Eve. My heart skips a beat as I realize what she means.

"You don't think—" I begin.

"The girl from the bombing!" she exclaims.

I shove the evidence bag into my case and close it. "We need to get to the security camera footage right now," I say.

"You think Danvers will give us access to it?" she asks.

"Let's hope so." I sling my bag over my shoulder, and we run down the hallway and back to the lobby, where Agent Danvers is talking to a group of agents whose badges all read FBI. I can't help but notice that she looks a hell of a lot more stressed than when we last saw her.

"Agent Danvers," I say as we reach her. "My partner and I need access to the security footage."

Agent Danvers murmurs something to one of the agents and turns to us. "What makes you say that?" she asks.

"We believe that the person who was here may be related to another case we are working on," Nicki says.

Agent Danvers appears almost bored with our request. "The footage is highly classified," she says. "I cannot simply give it to anyone who asks."

"Have you seen it?" Nicki asks.

"As a matter of fact, I have," Agent Danvers says. "Now get back to your assigned work."

"We know about the girl," I say. Agent Danvers' expression changes immediately. "We think she could be related to the bombing in Nashville a few days ago."

Agent Danvers turns to the FBI agents and says something I can't hear. They scatter, and Agent Danvers ushers Nicki and me into a room down a hallway. The room is dark, and when she turns on the lights, I see that it has carpet flooring, a wooden table, and plastic water cups. A break room.

"You two cannot just go around talking about her!" she snaps at us. "Imagine if the entire world knew that the U.S. government's most impenetrable facility was taken down by a child!"

"You didn't know this when we first came," I say, trying to make my voice sound calm, as if I was on top of everything.

Agent Danvers sighs. "No. I didn't. We'll have to get everyone who knows to sign NDAs so they keep their mouths shut."

"So you're not going to release all the facts to the papers?" Nicki asks.

"Well, when something like this happens, you have to be prepared not to. But this in particular...it's like nothing I've ever seen before."

"We will sign anything you want us to," I say. "But we need to see the footage. This girl, we think she could be related to the bombing in Nashville that occurred just two days ago."

I can see that she is considering it. After a few moments she opens the door and says, "Follow me." She walks us down several hallways to a small black door. Most of the other doors in the facility are a sleek gray color, but this one is jet black. She opens the door and leads us in. The room has at least a dozen large screens on one wall that show different views of Fort Knox. There are two other agents in the room dressed identically to Agent Danvers, except she has a few more badges and medals pinned to her uniform. I'd guess that they work under her. There is also a guy with his hands all over the keyboards; it looks like he's accessing the footage. When we walk in, they look more than a bit shocked to see us.

"Don't worry," Agent Danvers says. "They're with me. They want to see the footage of the break-in. Particularly the girl. They are only here to positively ID her—she might be associated with another case."

"That's the issue," the guy at the keyboard says. "Whoever broke in disabled the majority of the security cameras. The only ones active were the hidden ones on the ceiling that operate on a completely different system from the rest. It will be difficult to get a clear shot of anyone's face." He types something onto the keyboard, and the footage pops up. I immediately recognize it as the hallway outside the room the gold was stolen from. It is an aerial view, just as the man said. Standing at the door is a man with a tablet connected to the control panel that opens the door. There is a female standing behind him. It's tough to determine her age from this angle, but her hair certainly matches the girl from the bombing. I look at Nicki.

"Is this the girl you are looking for?" Agent Danvers asks.

"Hard to tell," I say. "We can't see her face."

"Try to get a shot of her face," Agent Danvers tells the guy at the keyboard. He fast-forwards the footage and pauses it just as a guard walks up to the girl.

"Why only one guard? You have dozens in here," Nicki asks.

"We had an imposter guard," the guy at the computer says. "He was working with the criminals that broke in. Together they took down the majority of the guards. We had a new squadron of guards come in today, and they were able to hijack them as well." He unpauses the footage, and the guard hesitates at the sight of the girl. I'm about to ask why, then I realize it must be because of her age. She moves toward him, pushing the gun out of the way and kneeing the guard in the groin. He doubles over and reaches for his taser, but he doesn't get a steady grip on it before the girl knees him in the head. He attempts a punch, but she dodges it quickly and grabs his gun from the floor where it fell. She picks it up backward and knocks him out with the butt of the gun. He falls to the floor.

I stand there, stunned. This minor took down a highly trained guard. Whether she's the kid from the bombing or not, a kid took that guard down. Something about that thought makes me sick to my stomach. The man fast-forwards again, and in a blur she takes down two more guards. I can sense Agent Danvers growing uneasy.

"Can you positively identify her?" she asks.

I glance at Nicki and can tell our answer is unanimous.

"No," I say. "It's hard to tell without a side-by-side comparison with a clear shot of her face. However, there certainly are resemblances."

Agent Danvers hastily whispers something in the tech guy's ear, and the screen goes black.

"We have some papers for you to sign," she says, turning toward us. "We will contact you if we find a clear shot of her face." She hastily ushers us out the door.

CHAPTER NINE

KENDALL

It's been four days since Fort Knox, and we are finally back at Alejandro, Eduardo, and Cecelia's home in the woods of Tennessee. We dropped the rest of the gang off in town, where most of them live, and they've taken the gold they picked up at Fort Knox with them. Our rules were clear: you take what you can fit into your pack. However, their spending will be limited, and they are not allowed to put any more than they normally might in the bank. This will limit the odds of their riches tying back to us.

I open the car door. It feels like years since I've been back here, and any thoughts of my past are wiped from my mind as I step out of the car and inhale the scent of the pine air. It's nice after an adventure like this to be back somewhere familiar. My leg is still tender and hard to walk on, but it will heal. I just stand there for a moment, taking it all in. The woods are really a magical place. The house is a small cabin with a satellite dish. Nothing special, but good enough for the four of us and Milo to stay in. This is the one place that I can truly say I like.

I hear the sound of claws clacking on the deck and look up to see Milo. I smile, and he comes bounding toward me. I pet him with my good hand and look up to see Cecelia. Cecelia is a small Mexican woman with long hair and the warmest smile you could imagine. I go over to her. She reaches out and gives me a side hug with her left arm, which she knows is the only type of hug I will accept.

"How was the trip?" she says. "The boys didn't give you too much grief, did they?"

"No, they were fine," I say.

"Good," she says. "Because I made food, and I'd hate for the two of us to be the only ones to enjoy it."

"You know you could never keep me away from food," Alejandro says, getting out of the van. Cecelia walks over to him and gives him a kiss on the lips.

"You would once I was through with you," she says. He laughs and gives her a hug. She gives me a small wink, and I smile again. We did it. A year's worth of planning to get into Fort Knox, and now it's over. We're home safe. It's weird. I expected relief. Feeling like I can rest. But right now all I feel is restless. Like I haven't done nearly enough for my plan. I want to kick myself. Jesus, what the hell is wrong with me?

Eduardo gets out of the car, without acknowledging Cecelia. Nonetheless, she drags us all inside. Cecelia and Eduardo don't really have the best relationship. They constantly argue and start conflicts over seemingly trivial things. Once Eduardo even threatened to shoot her when he was drunk. He didn't have any weapons on him, and he never actually hurt her, but I knocked him out anyway. I'm fairly sure he doesn't remember, but Cecelia sure does. We all try to keep him away from alcohol now.

We come in, and there is a feast prepared. Cecelia never fails to remind me of her talents in the kitchen. On the table are a dozen different Mexican dishes that I couldn't name if I tried. I just know they all taste good. And of course, there is my personal favorite on the side, which is the special Mexican rice she makes. I couldn't cook to save my life, so I have no idea what she puts in it, but whatever it is makes it turn orange and taste absolutely incredible. I never had food like that when I was younger. Almost everything I had was salvaged, and back then getting a greasy McDonald's was a treat. And I mean the cheapest thing you could buy at McDonald's. I don't think I've had a single fast-food meal since I've started living with the three of them, because Cecelia insists on cooking everything from scratch. She says it reminds her of what her mom would do for her when she was a little girl. It seems like a lot of work just to get a home-cooked meal, but I won't complain, because Cecelia's food is ten times better than anything we could ever get from eating out.

I begin to help Cecelia get out silverware until she sees what happened to my wrist and insists that I wait at the table. I know that she's trying to look out for me, but somehow it just annoys me.

"I'm gonna go outside," I grumble. I open the front door, and Milo follows me out. I sit on the steps of the deck and rest my leg. I properly bandaged it up and sanitized it. It didn't feel good, but I did it, and it's still sore. The cold winter breeze hits me immediately. I look up at the trees and stroke Milo's head. I look at the birds flapping their wings, the squirrels scampering from branch to branch. I wonder how they must feel. Meaningless? Unburdened? Free? What must it be like to be nothing to the world? To know that no matter what you did, it would have no effect on anyone but yourself? I guess I'll never know. My whole life is one big job now. And I will never forgive myself if I don't die accomplishing it.

I stroke Milo and hear the clanging of dishes inside. Cecelia must be done setting the table. Despite my annoyance at her, I feel like I haven't eaten in days, so I go inside. Everyone else is already helping themselves to the food. I grab a plate and do the same. I put a few dishes that look the best onto my plate. And of course, I scoop a large portion of rice as well.

I sit down and begin to eat. I try to eat slowly so I can enjoy the food, but once it enters my mouth, I wolf it all down in an instant. I get up to get more rice. Milo follows me and gives me those big puppy eyes of his. Cecelia tells me not to give in to his begging, but I'm sure a little bit of normal food won't hurt him. I pick up two pieces of flank steak while Cecelia isn't looking and "accidentally" drop them under the table. I feel better about eating my food if I know Milo's eating too. I sit down again to finish my rice.

~

After the sun has gone down, I head over to the computer in what we call the junk room. It doesn't really have a designated purpose; we basically just throw a bunch of random stuff that has no real place in the house in there. Calling it the junk room also makes it the perfect place for a set of false floorboards with a compartment underneath. We are hiding our share of the gold there until we can get it traded for money on the black market. But really, it could be used for anything. Hiding gold, weapons, even people. I take a seat on the chair in front of the desk. It has a bunch of random shit on it, such as old clothes and pens that no one knows the origin of, but there are two important things on it: the computer that we all share, and Eduardo's personal computer. He uses it for information, black market deals, and hacking. No one uses it but him, and I would complain about it if I had any idea how to use it. Honestly, even if he did let me use it, I would have no idea what to do with it. I make a mental note to make him teach me one of these days. It's not like he's going to be around forever.

I open the computer, and the screen lights up. I sign in and open the search engine that Eduardo set up. He installed some kind of software so no one can check our searches after we're done. That way if we look up anything connecting to a crime, or something the police would want to see, it will only be available to them when we are actually looking it up. As soon as we close out of the tab, no one will ever be able to see it again, and the IP address becomes untraceable. Another nice thing that he did was creating software to further categorize our searches.

The first thing I look up is "Mors Clan." My stomach twists into knots as I type in the name, and I have to resist the urge to actually hit myself. I am not afraid of them. I put in the "recent" filter to get a more specific search, and the first things that come up are an article about a bank they were suspected of robbing two months before the bombing in Nashville and another that talks about organized crime in the United States. I scroll down and see that there is nothing more recent. I relax a little. At least the plan is working somewhat. Then I clear the search and type in "Fort Knox." I don't add any filters. There are hundreds of articles out already, and it was only a few days ago. It looks like the story got out almost immediately. The American government prides itself on being democratic and free, but that stuff also prevents them from covering certain things up. Freedom of the press. It doesn't say anything about the perpetrators, which means one of two things: everyone who remembers us is dead or has a bad concussion, which sounds doubtful in my mind; or, the more likely scenario, the U.S. government doesn't want the public to know that they got their asses handed to them by a kid and a bunch of illegal immigrants. This is disappointing, to say the least. I was never in it for the money. All I wanted was to be recognized for it but not identified by the law. Hence the lack of a face mask. However, they can't keep it under wraps for long. They can't keep *me* under wraps for long. There were at least sixty witnesses who saw me at Fort Knox. One of them will have to speak up eventually. I smile. The plan is working perfectly.

CHAPTER TEN

DANIELLE

It's been almost a week since Fort Knox. The country has mourned the loss of the soldiers, and the United States government has mourned losses of its own. Its most secure facility is now being compared to a mere bank, and the people who worked there directly are utterly and completely humiliated. It reminds me of the story of Alcatraz, the prison that everyone thought nobody could ever escape from, but once one person figured out how, more followed. I can only hope that won't be the case this time. However, this being a one-off seems unlikely, since only a small portion of the larger stash was taken, leaving plenty for future criminals to take.

I find myself fingering my necklace—a thin metal rectangle with my name engraved on it. I got it for my eighteenth birthday. Almost ten years ago now. How could it have been so long since my sister pulled out that box and said she couldn't believe how old I was? I never had this habit before—well, I'd really rather not think about it right now. So much can change in three months.

However, dwelling on the past and a case that might not even connect to mine will accomplish nothing. I'm still at work, and I have a case to solve. Maybe the biggest case of my career, even if it isn't connected to the break-in at Fort Knox. I should be focused on that. The FBI hasn't so much as sent me an email since the break-in, so I can only continue the case as if there is no connection.

I decide to walk over to the crime lab. Detectives don't usually spend a lot of time there. If we ever interact with CSIs at all, it's usually if they come to us. However, I'm running on no evidence and no leads other than an FBI agent who may or may not even contact me.

So I walk over to where Darius is typing away on his computer. I could never do a job as tedious as a CSI again. I love the thrill of the mystery and the satisfaction of catching a criminal. I used to hate examining the evidence of a case as a CSI only to hand it off to a detective and never knowing the outcome of my work.

"How are we doing on the residue of the bombing?" I ask Darius. I've told Darius about the pictures of the girl with her dog, but I didn't mention that she could be connected to the Fort Knox break-in. All those documents we signed made sure that I couldn't say a word about that to anyone besides Nicki.

"Nothing incriminating," he says, referring to the girl. "And no human tissue or blood residue from the back side of the van."

In other words, there were no more dead bodies. "So the girl didn't die in the explosion."

"Well, I wanted to be sure, so I also looked for animal tissue or animal blood. There was none," he says.

"So the girl's dog couldn't have died in the explosion either," I say, more to myself than Darius.

"That's right," he says. Gears begin to turn in my mind. The girl must have gotten away before the explosion.

"Thank you," I say and begin to walk out of his lab.

"Where are you going?" he asks.

"Back to the crime scene," I say. "I need to see something."

~

I sit in the police car with the laptop on my lap. The area of the bombing is still surrounded with yellow tape, but there are no law enforcement officers at the scene. I pull up the picture of the girl in the alleyway. I look over to the alleyway across the street from where I'm parked. It seems to match the picture.

I get out of the car and walk across the street to the alley-way. It doesn't have much lighting, but it is still intact after the bombing. I look around, holding my laptop in one hand. I don't really know what I'm looking for. I guess I was just hoping to find something incriminating. Something that would *prove* that this girl was involved in the bombing somehow. But of course, I find nothing.

I walk out of the alleyway and down the sidewalk where the girl must have jogged past the van. I duck under the caution tape and past the significant crater that marks the spot where the van was. I walk around the corner and past the ruined building. How could she have gotten away before law enforcement arrived?

I keep walking and come to a dilapidated-looking dog park. It's less than a quarter mile from the crime scene, and no one is here. It appears that no one has been here in quite some time. Yellow tape put up after the bombing surrounds the parking lot, similar to other buildings in the area.

I scan the area and notice something. Tire tracks in the dirt parking lot. I bend down and examine them. They're no more than a week or two old. But no one could have entered with a car without ripping the caution tape. So if no one has been here for weeks...these tire tracks perfectly coincide with the time of the bombing. I think back to Jessica Owens' account of the man walking to a van identical to the one at the explosion site. Could this have been the van? I examine the tracks. They're about the right girth for a van the size of the one in the picture. I pull out my phone and text Nicki to send a sketch artist over to Jessica Owens' house and get all the details of her encounter with this man. Then I call Darius.

"Hey, Darius," I say. "I may have found the tire tracks of a getaway vehicle. I'll send you the location. Meet me here."

CHAPTER ELEVEN

KENDALL

Alejandro and I get out of the car and walk into the shop. It looks like a normal store. Shabby, but normal. The door jingles as we open it, and I look around. I think it's a furniture and home store. It sells silverware and other things that people use around the house. I look around a bit and see a shelf with books on it. I pick one up and see that it's a children's book. *Goodnight Moon*, it says on the cover, with a picture of a moon. So stupid. People raise their kids telling them that the world is perfect, people are perfect, everything is all sunshine and rainbows. No one tells their kids that people can hurt them. People can kill them. No one tells their kids that one day they might fall down and never get up. Stupid kids and their stupid parents. I look down on those kids for being so ignorant.

I put the book back, disgusted with it. I follow Alejandro to the cash register in the back. Bradley is standing behind the counter. He grew up with Alejandro and Eduardo, and I've known him for as long as I've known them. The criminal underworld can be a cruel and unforgiving place, and he is one of the only people we can trust. He isn't exactly a law-abiding citizen, but he is an honest businessman. And he knows how to keep a secret. When he sees us, a smile comes over his face. Not a kind one, but a knowing, funny smile. The kind you might give someone when you have an inside joke.

"Congratulations on your success," he says in his voice that always sounds like he's manipulating someone. That's one of the things that makes him so good at what he does. Just sounding like you're bending someone to your will asserts dominance over them. Even if all you're doing is telling them how nice the weather is today.

"Thank you," Alejandro says. "Congratulations on the new shop."

"Well, thank you," Bradley says. "I've been trying to...well, build." Bradley runs one of the biggest black-market shops in the Nashville area, and he's been talking about getting a normal shop for years now. It pretty much kills two birds with one stone. You can sell the things in your shop and have a place to run the black-market business. Having a fixed location puts you on the map.

"It looks good," Alejandro says. I nod in agreement, not wanting to be rude during a business exchange.

"Let's go back," Bradley says. "Shall we?"

We follow him behind the counter and behind a curtain where it looks like there are more goods. There are stacks of boxes lining the walls and an emergency exit at the end of the room. I remember what Ma'am taught me: never turn your back to an entrance if you're somewhere unfamiliar. So I stand with my back to the wall in between the two exits so that I can see them both. If you know where people can come in from, you will never be caught off guard.

Alejandro's eyes dart around for a bit before he seems satisfied that no one else is in the room. He sets down the black bag he has been carrying and opens it. There in the bag is our cut of the gold. Bradley smiles. Bradley is the only person outside of the gang who knows about the heist. In addition to helping us out, he charges extra for his silence. He doesn't tell anyone about his other customers—even Alejandro, who he's known for years. All for the right price, of course.

"We need you to exchange this for money," Alejandro says.

"And?" Bradley asks knowingly. "What's in it for me?"

"And we need you to melt down the gold," Alejandro says. He picks up a gold bar and turns it over to reveal a six-digit code on the back. "We need to get rid of the code. We'll give you a portion of our earnings."

"Hmm..." Bradley considers it. "It will cost you." Obviously. We just said that's what's in it for him. He pauses, and there is silence between the three of us.

"Fifty percent," he says finally. Fifty percent?!

"Tell him he's dreaming," I snap at Alejandro.

"So she speaks!" Bradley says. I glare at him and feel Alejandro glaring at me in return. I don't care. Bradley has heard me speak, first of all, and second of all, there is no way that we are giving him fifty percent of the take.

"Now, be nice, Kendall," Alejandro says.

I have to physically bite my tongue to keep myself from saying something that would probably get both of us kicked out of here. Alejandro turns to Bradley.

"Fifteen percent," he says.

"No less than twenty," Bradley says. "I only have so much untraceable laundered cash, you know." He sounds out the words "untraceable" and "laundered" slowly, as if trying to make them sound like paradise rather than a felony. "You have millions worth in that bag of yours. Plus, it won't hurt you to make an old friend rich. Better for my business, and in turn, better for you." I can see Alejandro considering it, and he mouths something that I can't read. I think he's doing the math to see how much we'll have left if Bradley takes twenty percent. A single bar of gold at Fort Knox is worth around $600,000. Between Alejandro, Eduardo, and me, we have twenty bars. That's about $12,000,000. If Bradley took twenty percent, he would be taking over two million dollars from us.

Just before I can tell Alejandro to say no, he speaks. "Fine," he says. "Deal."

"Wonderful!" Bradley says. He turns around and begins to open and go through a box. Alejandro picks up the gold and walks over to me.

"Behave yourself, kid," he whispers harshly. "Remember, Bradley's our friend."

"He's also a businessman," I retort. "One who is trying to squeeze money out of us."

Alejandro sighs. "You might be right about that, but try to act civilly. Don't always let your emotions get the best of you."

I gape at him and feel my hands turning to fists in my pockets.

"I'm sorry, who pulled off this amazing heist? Who had the grand plan that made you rich? Not your dumb ass. Don't act like you have anything to teach me."

"All I'm saying is don't be so angry with everyone all the time," he says. "We took you in, remember? We work well together, and we don't ask questions. The least you can do is be respectful."

"You first," I snap back. The remark feels childish, but it's all I can muster. I usually turn to using my fists before words at times like this. Alejandro doesn't have time to say anything before Bradley turns around and hands us a thick wad of cash. Alejandro counts the cash then hands him the bag of gold.

"Pleasure doing business with you," Bradley says.

"Always," Alejandro responds.

CHAPTER TWELVE

DANIELLE

I pick up Layla's ball for about the hundredth time in the past hour and throw it across the yard. Layla becomes a brown-and-white streak as she races across the yard to get it and then bounds back to drop it at my feet. I pick it up and throw it again. I love being outside, and it's finally a decent day. This will likely be one of the last weekends when I'm not working. There's always a pattern. I take a vague interest in a case, then I start to get into it, I start to get to know the victims, I start to get to know the perpetrator, and after that there's almost nothing that can drag my attention away from the case until it's solved—not even sleep. Before I know it, days, even weeks have passed before I either solve or give up on the case. But this case seems to be skipping all the steps. Each case has its own surprises, and this one has no shortage. The government could take it: If my perpetrator was the same person that broke into Fort Knox, I'm sure they would want an FBI agent on it, rather than a detective from Nashville. And to top it all off, the only suspect I have is a kid. That damn kid.

"So, are we gonna talk?" Jason asks, walking out the back door to meet me. "About everything?"

"About what?" I ask.

"Well, I dunno," Jason says. "You seem off since Fort Knox."

"Pretty brutal," I say blandly. "Lots to unpack."

"Is that what you're so upset about?" he asks.

"I'm not upset," I flat-out lie. "Who told you that?" He looks me in the eyes.

"Dani," he says. "We just got married last fall. A little honesty would be nice."

I sigh. "Alright, look, all I can tell you is that one of the people that broke into Fort Knox could be related to a case I'm working on."

"Damn," he says. "Which case?"

"That's classified," I say.

"But I'm your husband," he says. "And I'm a fellow law enforcement officer."

"Look, I can't tell you anything," I say. "I had to sign an NDA, and if Agent Danvers finds out I told anyone, she might not give me the information. This could really help my case, Jason! I thought you of all people would understand that!"

Jason puts his hands up as if surrendering. "OK! Sorry!"

We stand in silence and watch Layla playing with her ball for a moment. I suddenly feel guilty. Jason was only worried for me, and I shut him down. This situation isn't really fair to either of us. Before the feds got involved in the bombing case, I told Jason everything. He was my confidant, and I was his. If I'm being honest, keeping all this from him has been eating at me.

"OK, look..." I say. Jason turns to me with a teasing, smug smile, as if he knew all along I would open up to him. I give him a playful slap on the arm. "Shut up."

"I'm listening," he says.

"What I'm about to tell you," I begin, "you cannot tell anyone. You understand?" He nods, his face now serious. I begin to lower my voice. "The government wants this completely under wraps, but one of the people who broke into Fort Knox..." I pause. Once I tell him this, there's no going back. "...was a minor."

"What?!" he exclaims, leaning in closer, as if he could not have possibly heard me right.

"There was a young girl with the group that broke into Fort Knox. Looked maybe fourteen or so."

I pause as Jason processes this. His expression is a mix of shock and confusion. "A kid? Like just walking around with them?"

"No!" I whisper-yell. When the word comes out, I realize I sound just as shocked and confused about all of this as Jason does. "She was going along with it! And not only that, she was kicking their asses! These highly trained military guards got the living shit beat out of them by her! I saw the footage." Saying it out loud makes me intensely angry for some reason. I suddenly hate that girl. It takes more control than I expect to keep my voice down, but I manage.

Jason doesn't say anything for a long time. "Wow," he says quietly. "I can see why the government wants that under the radar. What could humiliate them more than having their best soldiers getting beaten by a kid?"

"Do you think that was purposeful?" I ask, feeling myself beginning to talk faster. "Train a kid, make the government lose face? It could explain why none of them were wearing face coverings. How else would we know it's a kid?"

"Maybe," he concedes, still seeming lost in thought. "How is she connected to the bombing downtown?"

"We got lucky," I say. "Nicki found a photographer that was taking pictures around the time of the bombing."

"And she was in the pictures?" he asks.

"Yes," I say. "The last one was taken just seconds before the bomb went off, and she is in it. She's jogging, with a dog, and she's the only person that's even remotely close to the bomb. She was in an earlier picture too, but that one's not as incriminating. After the bomb went off, she wasn't interviewed, and she wasn't among the injured or deceased. I checked missing persons reports, arrest records—there was no trace of her after that."

"Until Fort Knox," he says.

"Yes, but we don't even know if it's the same girl," I say. "They have the same general description, but there's no way to know for sure unless Agent Danvers comes back to me with clearer security footage."

"What does your gut tell you?" he asks. During cases, I've always had this intuition, this gut feeling that tells me what to do. I try to stick to the facts, but Jason always tells me to trust my gut, something I have rarely done.

I hesitate. "I think that it's the same girl," I say. "I mean, how many kids that age, fitting that description, are going to commit these major crimes?"

"Not many," he says.

"Exactly," I say. "I'm just shocked that a kid so young could do something like this."

"Kids are impressionable," Jason says. "You teach them right from wrong over and over from a young age, they'll believe it. Even if you tell them it's right to kill someone."

I nod. "I know I was resistant, but I'm glad I talked to you about this."

"Me too," he says, smiling. The sun is beginning to set, and a cold breeze blows through our backyard. I shiver. "What do you say we go inside and have some you and me time before you dive back into this case?"

I smile. "I'd like that." He gives me a quick kiss and holds me at arm's length.

"Hey, I know it's been a little tougher since, well, you know, Amanda and everything, and I just wanted to tell you how proud I am of you. You're so strong," he says. The mention of Amanda feels like a gut punch. On top of all of this, I am reminded yet again that my favorite person in the world is gone. And it's my fault. It's always been my fault. I want to throw up. I'm not strong. I'm awful. "This is all going to work out. I can feel it." I just nod again.

"I hope so," I say. "And thank you." I lean in and kiss him one more time before we walk inside.

CHAPTER THIRTEEN

KENDALL

I open my eyes to see the sun's rays beaming through my window. It always shines into my room in little slits because I boarded up the windows. I also always lock my bedroom door and place my little nightstand in front of it. That way, if someone opened it, the nightstand would fall, waking me up. I'm a light sleeper, so it would work. Eduardo calls me paranoid; I call myself prepared. I sit up and look around my room. It's not very big. In fact, it might as well be a walk-in closet, since there's barely enough room for the nightstand and my small bed. It's mine, though. Before I lived with Alejandro, Cecelia, and Eduardo, I'd never had my own room. Or anything of my own. Now I have my own room and an entire duffel bag with my own clothes, toiletries, and all of Milo's toys. It isn't much, but it's mine.

Milo, already awake, paws at me, asking me to pet him. He always sleeps at the foot of my bed. I obey and scratch behind his ear. He leans into my hand, and I know that means he likes it. It makes me laugh a little. I grab my duffel and walk to the bathroom. Milo follows me as I quickly clean my teeth and change into my clothes for the day. I don't have many clothes. Maybe about five sets altogether, but that's good enough for me. Today I put on my jeans, my blue t-shirt, and my gray sweatshirt. My main outfit for this time of year. I run a comb through my hair and put it up in a ponytail. I glance at myself in the mirror. Every time I look at my reflection, I can't believe how old I look. How different I look.

I walk out of the bathroom and into the kitchen, where Cecelia is washing dishes. She looks up when I walk in and smiles at me.

"Hey, honey," she says. "Are you hungry? We have some left-over breakfast."

"No, thanks," I say, grabbing an apple off the counter. "Not really a breakfast person."

"I know," she says.

"Where are Alejandro and Eduardo?" I ask.

"Running errands," she says. "Should be back by lunch."

"OK, sounds good," I say. "Is there anything you need me to do today? I know the water heater has been acting up; I can fix it if you need."

"No, Alejandro plans to fix it when he gets back," Cecelia says. "Do you have any plans for today?"

"I'd like to go on a hike with Milo," I say. "If that's OK with you."

"Yes, of course!" she says, then laughs. "Honey, when I was your age, I would go out with mi amigas and smoke weed." She laughs again. "You don't need my permission to go out and take a hike."

I laugh. "Thanks, Cecelia," I say. "I'll try to be back by lunch."

"OK!" she says. "I'm going to go read a book or something. Have fun!"

She gives me a wave before walking out of the kitchen and disappearing into her room. I walk over to the bathroom where I left my duffel. I get my winter gloves and hat out and put them on. I then grab Milo's leash and shove it in my sweatshirt pocket. I never use Milo's leash on hikes because he always stays close to me. However, I always take it so that if something happens and he's in a panic, I can strap it on and he won't run off. I then walk over to the front door, where my hiking boots are. I have two pairs of shoes: my hiking boots and a pair of black tennis shoes. I put on my hiking boots, and once Milo sees that I'm by the door, he prances over to me with his tail wagging.

"That's right, buddy, we're going on a hike," I say, scratching his neck.

Milo's smart, and when he hears the word "hike," his ears perk up. He knows what it means. When I first rescued him, I never suspected he was so smart. When I first found him, I was on the run. He was dumb, small, and vulnerable. Like I was. Maybe that's what motivated me to give him my food that night. And the night after that. And the night after that. Before I knew it, he was following me around. When I came to live with Alejandro, Cecelia, and Eduardo, he came with me. Dogs are so simple. You feed them, you give them a place to sleep, you pet them, and they love you unconditionally. Humans, on the other hand, are so complex, I couldn't even begin to try and understand them.

I open the front door, and Milo runs out. I follow him, and when he gets to the bottom of the porch stairs, he looks at me expectantly. I walk down the steps and decide to hike the big hill today.

I begin the route, and Milo immediately knows where we're going. He begins to walk about twenty yards in front of me, sniffing every tree stump, dead leaf, and rock. I follow him and check my watch: 8:03 a.m. That should give us plenty of time to make it to the top of the hill and back before lunch. We might even have some time to play fetch or something when we get to the top.

As we begin walking, I look around. I've always loved how alive the woods are. How the birds always chirp, the wind always blows, the leaves are always rustling. Yet there's always a sense of peace here. Like maybe this is the one place in the world where I belong.

I can't help but think how much Natalie would have loved this place. She, like me, always loved to be outside. Really, it was just an escape from home, but she saw the magic in it too. This...this life...it's all she ever really wanted for us. The simplicity, the peace —that's what she would always talk about.

A wave of guilt hits me. It sickens me to my stomach. Here I am. Living Natalie's dream life without her. I walk a bit faster, as if trying to outrun the thought. I want to kill someone. I hate this. I hate this guilt. I hate this sadness. I just want it to be over. But most of all, I hate being so helpless. I hate knowing that no matter what, there is nothing I can do to make myself OK again. There is nothing in this world that will bring Natalie back.

All I can do now is avenge her.

CHAPTER FOURTEEN

DANIELLE

I walk to the station with Nicki. Morning coffee is kind of our thing. It helps to get to know your partner outside of work, especially in law enforcement. If you're going to catch criminals and be in high-pressure situations together, there has to be trust. And to trust each other, you have to know each other. Nicki and I have been working together for two years now, and I think I can safely say that I know her well. She's my best friend and was a bridesmaid at my wedding. My wedding. Again, I am confronted with the memory of walking down the aisle without Amanda watching. Without my maid of honor. I want to pity myself for it, but pity is the last thing I deserve. I don't want to think about it. I just need to focus on my job and this case.

"So, how's Jason?" Nicki asks, distracting me from my thoughts. "Is he still all stressed out with moving and everything?"

I laugh. "No, no, Jason's good," I say. "Especially since *I* have been doing most of the moving work." Nicki laughs.

"What about you?" I ask. "How's the new house?" Nicki moved out of her apartment and into a small suburban home about a month ago. It's the biggest place she's lived in on her own, so I've been over there helping her on our days off. That's one of the nice things about being partners—you get the same days off, because you work the same cases.

"The house is good," she says. "I finally got rid of the last of the boxes, so I am now officially moved in."

"Hey, that's great!" I exclaim.

"Yeah! I was happy about that!" she says. "But my plumbing system's still on the fritz."

"I've been telling you to get it looked at!" I say. "You never listen to me!"

"I will!" she says. "Eventually." I let out an exasperated sigh, and she laughs. "But you know, with this case and everything, I probably won't have time for things like that."

"Yeah, I know," I say. "It's crazy how big this whole thing has gotten."

"Yeah," she says.

I feel my phone vibrate in my coat pocket and pull it out. It's the chief. "Speaking of which," I say, hitting the green answer button and holding the phone up to my ear. "Hello, Chief Daley," I say. "I was under the impression that my shift didn't start for another twenty minutes."

"It's not that, Detective Toole," Chief Daley says. "An FBI agent is looking for you. Keeps calling your desk phone. She called me a minute ago. Do you know anyone named Agent Danvers?"

My heart skips a beat. "Yes. Yes, I do. We'll be there as soon as we can." I hang up and turn to Nicki.

"What was that?" she asks.

"It's Danvers," I say. "Chief says she's been calling. This could be our lead. We have to go."

~

Ten minutes later, Nicki and I are at the station. We practically run in the doors and up the stairs to my desk. I can only pray that we didn't miss our opportunity. Agent Danvers works for the FBI, and I'm sure calling two middle-grade detectives is low on her list of priorities.

When we get to my desk, I see three missed calls on my phone from an unknown number. God, I hope we're not too late. I pick up the phone and dial her number. It rings five times before she picks up. Nicki hovers beside me, waiting.

"Detective Toole," Agent Danvers says. "Glad I got hold of you."

"Agent Danvers," I say. "Thank you for calling me. I assume this means you have information for me?" I'm careful not to be too specific since there are a few officers in here, and I don't want to risk being overheard.

"Yes," she says. "We have gone over the security footage down to the millisecond, and we found a clear shot of the suspect's face. I emailed it to you."

I log in to my work computer and check my email. Sure enough, there is an email from Agent Danvers. I open it, and attached is a single picture. Judging from the distance the cameras were from the ground, this shot must have been zoomed in a lot, but it's still very clear. I pull the tab over to the left side of my screen and open the picture we have of the girl at the Nashville bombing. I pull that tab over to the right side of my screen and compare the two pictures side by side. I look at them for a long while. Same color hair, same hairline, same hazel eyes, same face shape. It is without a doubt the same person in both photos. My heart skips a beat as I realize what this means.

"It...looks like the same person," I say, almost not believing the words coming out of my mouth. I glance at Nicki, and she smiles at me. I smile back.

"That's good, Detective Toole. But I'll need you to email me the picture you have so I can get an expert opinion," she says. "That's the only way I can officially get you on this case. We'll have to work together on this if we want to catch this girl. I'll call you when I have what I need."

"OK, thank you," I say. I attach the image and hit send. "I sent it."

"Good," she says. "And there's something else."

"What is it?" I ask.

"The hair you found at the scene cannot be used directly for DNA analysis, as you know, but we did find blood at the scene," she says. "We know the hair is hers, and so we cross-referenced the DNA with the blood, and the blood is hers as well."

"Did you run it through the system?" I ask.

"Yes," she says. "There are no direct matches. Whoever this girl is, she has no arrest record."

"If there were no matches, why are you telling me this?" I ask.

"Because there were two matches with a similar DNA sequence in the bone marrow, meaning they share the same maternal DNA as our suspect," she says. "I'd like you to investigate them. I'm sending the information to you now."

"I'd be happy to, but I don't work for the FBI," I say.

"You have proven yourself useful, Detective Toole," she says. "We are short staffed as it is, and it is taking all our resources to locate the rest of the suspects from Fort Knox. Unlike the girl, we have no leads on them. If you and your partner can work with us on this, it could speed up our investigation, and we can catch these people as soon as possible. The news coverage of the break-in is already being minimized. The government wants this to go away as quickly as possible, and frankly, so do I. Don't worry, I'll help you out; I just need someone to do the legwork."

"Yes, ma'am," I say. She hangs up, and I turn to Nicki and quickly relay all the information to her.

"I can't believe it. This is great. Now we're not only going to have more evidence, but we're going to have the federal government and its resources helping us on this case."

"I know," I say. "I think this is our big break."

CHAPTER FIFTEEN

KENDALL

The rest of the hike, I am livid. I can hardly enjoy anything and decide to turn around early with Milo on my heels. I don't know exactly what could make me feel better back at the cabin, but a small voice inside me is saying that there is something. Either that or I just want to stay in my room, lock the door, and shove my feelings so deep down I forget they're even there. I'll figure it out when I get there. As I walk back down the hill, everything beautiful I see just reminds me that Natalie will never see it, and I keep walking. I finally reach the bottom of the hill, and I have just enough sense left to make sure that Milo follows me. When I see him trotting down the hill behind me, I continue into the cabin.

When I get inside, I finally know what I have to do. I run through the kitchen and into the junk room. I practically leap onto the chair and look up the same thing I did the night I returned from the job: the Mors Clan. I have to reassure myself that this plan is working. That I'm finally beating them, that I'm outshining them. That I'm foiling every plan they had.

But of course, with my luck, it is the opposite. A recent raid of a police station, a news article from just today pops up, with their name in the headline. My heart drops. My head starts pounding. No. No. This can't be right. They should be stopping. They should know that it was me who broke into Fort Knox. They should know that their life's goal is being destroyed by me, when they themselves destroyed me. I should be ruining them— Stop. I still could be.

I open a new tab and look up the Fort Knox break-in. There has to be more coverage on that, right? I mean, it's the crime of the century. The search loads, and nothing comes up. Nothing. I scroll through, and still nothing.

I run over to the living room and turn on the TV. I switch channels until the national news comes on. A woman with obviously bleached blonde hair begins talking about a series of cyclones in India. After about twenty minutes with no mention of the break-in at Fort Knox, I switch channels. Still nothing. I shut off the TV.

How can it not be in the news? How can it already have phased out of the news to the point that you can't even look it up? I mean, people have to be wondering what happened to all the news about it. It's only been about two weeks. People can't just forget about it that quickly.

And then it hits me. Maybe they haven't. This is a government cover-up. I bury my head in my hands. This is everything I feared. A year of work. *A year.* Just thrown down the drain because I hurt the American government's precious ego. How am I supposed to complete my plan? This was it. This was the big plan, and I messed it up.

No. I think to myself. *No. I didn't come all this way for nothing. There has to be something else I can do.*

The door opens, and I hear Eduardo's irritating voice. "Hey, woman! Why is our lunch not ready?"

I scowl at the thought of having to deal with him once more, but then the idea comes to me.

We have to find another job to complete my plan.

~

"No!" Alejandro yells. "Absolutely not!"

"Alejandro!" I argue. "The government is covering it up! Covering *us* up! What was the point of all this if we don't even get credit?"

"To make us rich!" Alejandro snaps. "And we are! But we paid the price! We all have a target on our back now! What makes you think they won't catch us the second we get a speeding ticket!"

"Because you have me!" I say. "I have been doing this my whole life! I know how to sneak around them so that they'll never catch us!"

"The whole world is looking for us!" Alejandro argues. "This was not the plan! We were supposed to lie low! Going on another job is suicide!"

"The plan wasn't for them to cover it up either!" I snap. Cecelia and Eduardo shift nervously off to the side. "Think about it! The public doesn't even know it was us! They're forgetting about it as we speak! The only way for us to stay relevant is to continue these jobs!"

"We have more money than we can spend in a lifetime," Alejandro says. "Staying relevant is not my goal. If they want to cover it up, fine! Let them! It works better for us anyway."

I really want to scream at him right now. We need the credit. I need the credit. How else will anyone ever know that it was me? How else will the only people that matter in all of this know it was me? But I can't yell at Alejandro. I can't risk exposing my motive. He could find it too petty and personal to be calculated enough.

I speak in a calm voice. "You have dedicated your life to this gang," I say. "You have been a criminal your entire life. You *want* the credit. I told you when I came here that this job could make your gang bigger than the Mors Clan." Make *me* bigger than the Mors Clan. "That's not possible now. Unless we do another job. Don't tell me you pulled the biggest heist in the world only to go all soft once it was over."

There is a long silence between us, and it feels as if the world has gone still. Eduardo and Alejandro share a knowing glance. I look from Eduardo to Alejandro and back again, trying to tell what they could possibly be thinking. Alejandro has to agree. Even though I would never tell him what it is, another job, another chance to get my picture into the headlines, potentially even my name, is the only way to complete my plan. If he doesn't agree, I'm not sure what I'll do.

"How would you propose doing another job?" he asks, his tone significantly calmer than just a few moments ago.

I breathe an internal sigh of relief. "Well, it would take some planning," I say. "But with our team, we could figure it out."

"Something smaller this time," Alejandro says. "Something that wouldn't get covered up but would still make the news."

I turn to Eduardo. "We'll need you to hack some stuff again." Eduardo nods, and I turn back to Alejandro. "We'll need to get the gang together as well. They need to be better prepared this time."

"Are you sure about this?" Alejandro asks.

I force myself to give him a reassuring smile. Although I'm not sure if it's for him or me. "After Fort Knox, this should be a piece of cake."

CHAPTER SIXTEEN

DANIELLE

"So did Agent Danvers say anything other than the location of the first DNA match?" Nicki asks as she makes a right turn onto the interstate.

I open up my laptop to check the data she sent me. "Well, it's in the Arkansas state morgue, so it's a dead body."

"Right," she says. "And where's the second one?"

I check my laptop again. "The state prison."

"So we have one relative in prison and one dead." Nicki half chuckles and half scoffs. "Rough family."

"Yeah..." I say, continuing to read from my laptop.

"And the two matches were never connected?" Nicki asks. "The living one was never asked to identify the body?"

"They were," I say. "They were connected by the maternal gene, same as our suspect, meaning they are at least half siblings. The dead one was kept in the morgue because of her potential involvement with the Mors Clan. From the living one's own account, they were both part of it." Nicki nods, and I notice a shift in her expression at the mention of the Mors Clan. "You've heard of it?"

"Only whispers," she says and stares blankly at the road for a long time, as if deep in thought. "Before we were partners, back when you worked in the lab, for one of my first cases, I was investigating a homicide just outside the city. Duncan Williams. A man shot five times in his own home. The gun was left at the scene, with no fingerprints or DNA whatsoever. My old partner Detective Garcia and I had nothing to go on." I nod curiously. "That was, until a man ran into the station. He wanted to confess to a murder. Garcia and I got him into an interrogation room, and we asked him questions. He admitted to the murder of Williams, gave all the right details, including that the gun was left at the scene, a detail that wasn't released to the press. But something was off. He had no history of violence, mental illness, or any link to Williams at all. He had no motive. And more than that, he seemed...scared. I figured at the time it was because he just killed someone, but it didn't add up. Nonetheless, he knew details about the murder only someone who was there would know, so we placed him in a cell."

She pauses and fidgets with her rings nervously with one hand while the other hand clenches the wheel with pale knuckles. I quickly decide against pointing out her anxiousness aroused by the story and wait for her to continue.

"The next day we went in for round two, and he was practically shaking the entire interrogation. We went over details for about a half hour before he claimed that he didn't do it. He said that someone made him confess, and that he needed our help. We asked him who. He said the Mors Clan. That was the first time I'd heard of them. The next day when I walked into work, the station was in complete chaos. We found a liquid sedative in the coffee that the guards drank overnight, and the cameras had been disconnected. We found the man in his cell with his throat slit. No fingerprints, no DNA, no evidence as to who had done it. Just like the murder of Duncan Williams."

A vague memory of the station in complete disorder a few years ago surfaces in my memory. Somehow it makes the whole event seem more real. More terrifying. That someone could break into a police station and murder a prisoner without any evidence. It seems nearly impossible.

"They could have shot him. They could have killed him quickly, but they didn't. They didn't even slit the carotid artery. It took him two hours to bleed out. They wanted to make an example out of him. They wanted to make him suffer. It was the Mors Clan. Who else would have killed him? These people, Dani, they're monsters. They're everywhere, in everything."

I try to keep the growing wave of fear and uncertainty under control. I clear my throat. "So you're saying we should be careful when investigating these people?" I ask.

"I'm saying that if we get too close, if we step on the wrong twig here," she responds, "that twig could become a landmine. It could get very ugly for us, very quickly."

I find myself pulling up the picture of the girl's face from Fort Knox. The one that Agent Danvers emailed to me. I have more questions swirling around in my head than answers.

~

"How long have you had the body?" I ask the forensic examiner as I suit up to go into the body fridge. Morbid term, I know, but that's what it is. You have to keep the corpses cold to keep them preserved.

"This one..." he begins, flipping through the binder in his hands, "about two years. She died one to two weeks before that."

"Cause of death?" Nicki inquires.

"Three bullet wounds," he says. "One to the left leg, two to the back. It seems that she was running from whoever shot her."

"Where was the body found?" I ask.

"In some woods just outside of Saint Charles," he says. "A hiker found her."

"Alright, thanks," Nicki says, taking the binder from him. I put my mask over my face. "You ready?" I nod.

We walk into the freezer, and I immediately wish I had brought a sweatshirt. However, I can't focus on that because in the middle of the room, on a metal table, is the body. I try to put my mind into work mode. It's something I do whenever I get to a certain place in a case, or return to the scene of the crime, or most of the time when I look at bodies. I've gotten better at it in my years on the force. Now it's like flipping a switch. It helps me not to get too emotionally invested in cases. If I start to do that, I know I won't be able to continue my work.

That's why usually I'm not nervous about examining bodies. But this is the first one since...well, since the incident. I can feel a knot balling up in my stomach. I can already sense that this time will be different. I need to be able to continue this case. This isn't about me, I remind myself, this is about catching a criminal and getting justice for their victims.

I walk up to the body and thank god that they closed her eyes. She's young. I'd guess around eighteen to twenty. She has a sheet over her body, and her face is incredibly pale. I've never seen a body this old before. She doesn't have any hair, which is normal for a body that has been exposed to the elements for a few weeks. Some of her skin has decayed too, and there are places where you can see her bones and tissue.

I will myself not to think about the last time I saw a dead body. The day that my whole world came crashing down around me. But I can't. The moment I see the body, I think about her. Amanda. My sister. My best friend. My maid of honor.

I remember the day in the car.

I'm sitting in the driver's seat. We're going down 465. Seventy miles per hour. Amanda's in the passenger's seat, her feet up on the dashboard. It used to drive my mom crazy when she did that, which is why when I got my license she always wanted to ride with me.

"Dani, come on, it's not that hard," Amanda teases me and giggles. "Tulips or roses."

"It *is* that hard, Amanda," I retort. "This is going to be the biggest day of my life, and everything has to be perfect. Choosing which flowers we have is a big deal."

"Well, if everything needs to be so perfect, why did you pick me to plan it?" she teases.

"I'm dumb," I blurt out.

Amanda chuckles. "You said it, not me." I see something out of the corner of my eye: a truck. The driver appears intoxicated and is swerving across the highway.

"Woah." Amanda's tone turns serious. "Be careful, Dani. That guy—"

That's the last thing she said before that goddamn drunk driver rammed into the passenger side of my car. The world went blurry, and I couldn't focus. My car was pinned between the truck and the guardrail, keeping my car from sliding off the highway into a ditch. My windshield shattered, and Amanda vanished from my passenger seat. My sister. My best friend. My maid of honor.

I climbed through the windshield. I called her name. I found her on the side of the road. I ran to her and turned her on her back. Her eyes were fixed open. I had seen dozens of bodies before. I knew right then that she was dead, but I didn't want to accept it. I started chest compressions. Like they always taught us in training. Tears stung my eyes, but I didn't stop. I repeated the compressions until her ribs were broken, trying to undo my mistake. I was driving the car. I could have saved her. I kept pressing on her chest as if it could jerk her heart back into rhythm. Emergency services declared her dead on the scene. I screamed.

The sound of Nicki opening up the file pulls me back into reality. I clear my throat, not acknowledging the hot tears stinging my eyes.

"Estimated age?" I ask.

"Sixteen to twenty-two," Nicki says.

I pull the sheet off her chest and stomach and examine the bullet wounds. "The entry point was definitely from the back," I say. "Looks like the bullets didn't puncture any vital organs though, so she would have bled to death." I pull the sheet down past her legs so only her ankles are covered. "The third one also entered from the back." Then I notice something, faint scratch marks on her left knee. I point at them and glance over at Nicki.

She immediately looks down at the medical report and scans it. "There's no record of that on the report," she says. "The forensic examiner could have missed it; it's pretty faint."

"But this wasn't included in the original report," I say. "There's more to this girl's story."

"But what is it?" she asks. "What does this mean?"

"Well, it could be from someone trying to move the body after the murder. The forensic examiner said that a hiker found her, so whoever moved her either wasn't making an effort to hide her, or they didn't do a very good job. Wait..." I say. "Wait, look, there's only a skid mark on one knee."

"So?" Nicki asks.

"So she had to be walking with the other leg, or at least attempting," I say. "Whoever dragged her...they dragged her before she died. They were trying to help her." I feel my voice beginning to crack. A feeling of dread creeps into me. What is wrong with me?

"So there was a third person at the scene," Nicki says.

"That's right," I say, beginning to feel uneasy. I cover the body back up with the sheet, and I find my mind immediately going to the girl as we walk out of the freezer.

"Do you think it could have been the suspect? She was related to the victim," she says.

"It's possible," I say. "We shouldn't rule anything out too soon."

Somehow, that upsets me. Why does it upset me that something horrible happened to a horrible person? It's probably better, right? That she wasn't born horrible, but something made her that way. Or is that worse? That she was an innocent girl who was preyed upon again and again until there was nothing left.

No. I tell myself. I cannot let my emotions get the better of me in this case. *Especially* not in this case. I just need to catch this girl. It doesn't matter what happened to her to make her into a criminal; all that matters is that she is one. Now I have to do my job and catch her.

CHAPTER SEVENTEEN

KENDALL

We begin to get our gloves and masks on. It's only been a few days since I convinced Alejandro to go on a job, and we are already prepping. The job is today. It's amazing how much you can get done with the right group of people. We are going to be robbing the State Reserve Bank in Kentucky. We should be arriving there later tonight. However, this isn't just a normal bank. This is where rich people, and I mean like loaded people, keep their valuables and their kids' college funds.

We are in a dugout in a town on the outskirts of Nashville. It's kind of like our safe place. Alejandro and Eduardo created it before I even knew them. It's in an old unfinished basement, which is why there is no insulation and no finished walls. It's basically just a big hole in the ground with an old house over it. No one has come here in the years that we have been using it, so I feel fairly safe here.

As I put on the black gloves, I notice a few more people in the gang than last time. I've never been great at remembering people by their faces, but I can tell from the strange looks I've been getting that I've never met a good chunk of these people. I recognize a few faces, but the vast majority are completely foreign to me. I can feel my confidence in the gang begin to waver. Maybe I made the wrong choice. Alejandro is at Bradley's, purchasing last-minute supplies, and Eduardo is perfecting his hack of the bank's security cameras. In his words, "If I can get this right, those cameras will be down for days." I don't want to risk messing up his work, so I know I can't ask him about the extra people in the gang.

That's when I spot Juan. He's so stupid the thought of talking to him makes me want to physically gag, but I know that it's necessary. I walk over to him, and when he sees me, he gives me a sly smile. As if he's so smart and conniving. For god's sake, he's a drunk! I try to control the rage in my voice as I speak.

"Who are these guys?" I ask. "They weren't at Fort Knox."

"We're popular," he says, smirking at me like an idiot. "Everyone knows about the heist we pulled. When they heard that we were going on another, they all wanted in."

"Everyone knows?!" I ask, feeling my temper rising. "We are supposed to be keeping a low profile! We're trying to stay hidden and still be able to pull stuff like this off. You blabbing the entire thing to everyone you meet doesn't help!"

"Calm down!" he says. "Don't worry, I trust these guys. We hang out all the time, even before Fort Knox."

"Do you trust them with your life?" I ask accusingly.

Juan opens his mouth and hesitates for a moment before speaking. "Yes," he says.

"Good," I say roughly. "Because now my life depends on them too."

~

After about an hour, Alejandro finally returns with the supplies. It was mainly firearms off the black market. It was my plan to buy them the day of the job so that if anyone got suspicious of our connection to other crimes and got a warrant, we wouldn't have any firearms on us. We ditched the guns we brought to Fort Knox. We couldn't risk anyone tracking us. Our government tends to go all out when it comes to security, so there's no harm in being cautious.

Alejandro sets down his purchases on an old wooden table near the entrance of the dugout. It creaks as the heavy bags weigh it down. I make a mental reminder to get a new table before that one collapses. The gang members flock to the guns and ammo, and I'm beginning to think that maybe we should hold on to the guns until the job. I don't know any of these people, and they could easily betray us.

Alejandro seems to have the same thought, because he says, "Whoa! Whoa! Amigos! You may each take a gun of your choice, but ammunition cannot be taken until we get to the job site." I give him a nod of approval and wait for everyone else to choose their weapons before I get mine. I know that I'm a better shot than any of these people, so I don't need to be picky.

I walk up to the table, and there is one gun and holster left. I strap the holster to my jeans, and Alejandro hands me the short handgun. It looks familiar, but I can't quite place it. I take the gun and feel the weight of it in my hand.

"That's a .22 caliber magnum," Alejandro says. "Can you shoot with that?"

And then it's like I'm back there. I'm in the woods. Outside of my old house. I'm nine. The hostage is tied to a tree, a gray cloth bag over his head. I have been dreading this day for so long.

"Here you go," Sir says. "A .22 caliber magnum. Your favorite." He hands me the gun. The hostage seems to have heard that and begins to squirm and try to break free. I try to remind myself that this is a privilege. This is what I have wanted for years. A knot forms in my stomach. Just this morning this man was home with his family. He doesn't deserve to die.

My hand shakes as I raise the gun. I try to hold the bead on the man's chest, where his heart is, but I can't get my hands to stay steady. I'm going to kill someone. I'm going to take someone off this earth. I'm going to ensure that this man doesn't go back home to his family tonight. I can feel my breath quicken and my head begin to pound with the thought of all this. Panic begins to set in.

"Well, what are you waiting for, Kendall?" Ma'am asks. "Kill him." What is wrong with me? I had been so certain I would be able to do this. To kill someone. But now that he sits before me, entirely helpless, I'm not so sure.

"But Ma'am," I begin. "He hasn't done anything wrong." I regret the words as soon as they leave my mouth. The blow hits my face instantly, and I fall to the ground. Stars dance in front of my eyes.

"That kind of thinking makes you soft!" Ma'am yells. She kicks me in the stomach, making me cough and wheeze. "Kill him, dammit!"

My vision is going in and out of focus, and everything hurts. I struggle to sit up and catch Natalie's gaze on me. I can see the glint of concern in her eyes, but her expression is determined. She gives me a nod. I inhale sharply and, gun in hand, I get to my feet. I grunt as I lift the gun, sights aimed at the man's head, and all I can think about is the beating that will result if I fail a second time. I pull the trigger.

"Hey, kid," Alejandro says, a little louder. I flinch, realizing that I had probably just looked lost in thought to him. "I asked if you could shoot that gun."

I glance at the .22 caliber magnum in my hand. "Better than you'd think," I respond.

CHAPTER EIGHTEEN

DANIELLE

As I walk into the Arkansas State Prison, I am eager to listen to what this relative of the suspect has to say. What I am not eager about is the possibility of a long interrogation. Nicki called in sick today, which means I'll have to do the interrogation alone. Interrogations can take hours, and I am not looking forward to not being able to switch out with someone, or at least having someone else in the room I can trust. I guess I'll just have to deal with it. As long as it gets me closer to an answer on this kid, however long it takes, it will be worth it.

I walk to the front desk, where a very bored-looking police officer is sitting in front of a computer. "Are you a visitor?" she asks in a nasal voice.

"No," I say. "I have an interrogation with a prisoner. Andrea Cooper."

"May I see your badge and ID?" the woman asks. I hand her both over the counter, and she inspects them. She types on the computer keyboard for about a minute until she finally says, "OK, you're good." She hands me my badge and ID back. "You can go in that door over there." She points to a door to the left of the desk.

"Thank you," I say and begin to walk toward it. When I open the door, I see that I am in what looks like a waiting room for the dentist; it's the size of a closet. There are chairs lined up against the wall, and I take a seat. I wait for about ten minutes before a woman opens the door.

"Are you Detective Danielle Toole?" she asks.

"Yes," I say.

"Andrea Cooper is ready for you," she says. "I'll escort you to the interrogation room." I stand up and clench my briefcase in my hand. I follow the woman, who introduces herself as Officer Williams, to a door near the middle of the prison. "There will be officers monitoring your entire conversation. If you want to leave, I will be here waiting for you."

"Thank you," I say. I take a deep breath and open the door. The room is all white, like most interrogation rooms I've been in. There is a brown table with two glasses of water on it and a black plastic chair at either end. The one closest to the door is empty, and the one on the other side of the room has a woman in it. She looks a couple years younger than me, maybe in her early twenties, but there is something distinct about her demeanor, maybe the way she holds herself, the way she looks at me, that makes her seem much, much older. She has hair that might be a shade of dirty blonde, but it's so greasy and tangled that it's impossible to tell. Her eyes are a cold shade of gray that makes her expression difficult to read.

I make my way to the chair closest to the door. I take a seat and open my briefcase. I pull out the file I have on Andrea Cooper and open it.

"Let's make something clear, Ms. Cooper," I say. "You have already been sentenced to life in prison. You were originally arrested for aggravated assault at a bar, but you were soon connected to four counts of first degree murder and one count of arson, and I quote your words to your former cellmate: 'Those are just the things that they caught.' There is nothing that you can say or do in this interrogation that could lengthen your sentence."

Andrea smirks. "What's it to you, copper?"

I pull out the picture of the girl at Fort Knox on a full-sized piece of paper. It's the clearest picture we have of her. I pull out another picture, the same size and format as the first one, except it is of the unidentified body in the woods. The picture is the oldest picture taken of the body, so it should be the easiest for Andrea to recognize. That is, if she has any knowledge about what happened to either of them. I turn the images so that they are facing her.

"I'm looking for information," I say. Andrea doesn't even glance at the pictures on the table and stares me dead in the eyes.

"What's in it for me?" she asks.

"Well, as I said before, you have been convicted of several quite heinous crimes," I say calmly. "And as of right now, you have no possibility of parole." I can see her expression begin to shift. "You tell me everything you know, and you'll be able to leave the grounds again." I can see the longing in Andrea's eyes. I'm sure prison life gets boring, even lonely, for someone like her. This offer is sure to entice her. Andrea hesitates for a moment before speaking again.

"You've got yourself a deal," she says. I try not to let my relief show.

"What do you know about these two people?" I ask. She stares at the images for a moment, then a smile creeps across her face. She recognizes them.

"These two..." she says slowly. "I haven't seen them in a long, long time." Her expression is almost amused.

"Who are they?" I ask.

She takes her eyes off of the images and looks at me. "Their names are Natalie and Kendall Cooper," she says. She taps the picture of the body with her finger when she says Natalie and taps the picture of the girl at Fort Knox as she says Kendall. Natalie and Kendall Cooper.

"Cooper," I repeat. "What is your relation to them?"

"They were my sisters," she says, eyeing the pictures again. "Of course, sibling is a term you could throw around lightly in my house. I'm sure I have half a dozen siblings I didn't even know existed." Andrea chuckles. "These two didn't seem to realize that though. They were thick as thieves."

"Were?" I ask, as if I have no idea that Kendall Cooper is alive.

"Well, I *know* Natalie is dead," Andrea says. "I've always believed that Kendall would follow, but the little rat is stubborn. Ma'am always said that out of all us kids, she had the most potential." Andrea smiles again. "So either you don't have her and you want to catch her, or you have her and she's not talking."

"Are you willing to help us?" I ask, being careful not to say which one of her theories is true. Andrea runs her finger over Kendall Cooper's picture a few times before answering.

"To convict that little shit? Hell yeah, I'll help you." She pushes the picture of Kendall back toward me. So she didn't like her. I wonder why.

"Then tell me everything you know about her," I say, not softening my tone. "And Natalie Cooper."

"Well, as the people here already know, my family is part of a certain crime organization. The Mors Clan. I'm sure you've heard of it. It was gonna be the biggest name in America by the time I was an adult, they always said," she says. I can't help the lump in my throat when she mentions the Mors Clan. Nicki's story creeps back into my memory. I need more information from Andrea. "But before you ask, no, I have no idea where they are now. When one of their own gets arrested or killed, they pack up and leave no evidence. You couldn't catch them if you tried."

"And Kendall and Natalie Cooper were part of this organization?" I ask.

"Yeah," she says. "They were good, too. Especially Kendall, as Ma'am would remind me every day. But I guess they didn't appreciate their talent very much, because they ran away. Or at least they tried to." So she was jealous of Kendall.

"Ma'am is your mother?" I ask.

"Oh yeah," Andrea says. "That's what she had us call her. She was more our leader than our mother."

"So what exactly would they have you do in this crime organization?" I ask.

"Smaller assignments for the younger kids," she says. "Stealing firearms shipments for larger assignments, being a decoy, things like that. But for the older kids, they would go on the big assignments. Bank robberies, assassinations, taking hostages, all in the good name of the Mors Clan." Andrea leans back in her chair and folds her arms over her chest. She looks off into the distance, her eyes far away, as if she is remembering it. I can't tell if the memories dancing around in those gray eyes are good or bad.

I wonder if her parents were physically abusive. That couldn't be too much of a stretch considering they worked for a crime organization. It might also explain both her and Kendall's erratic behavior. Not to mention that they were both convicted or suspected of major crimes when they were just minors. I wonder if that is the sole cause.

"What would the punishment be if, say, you performed poorly on an assignment?" I question further. Most abuse victims aren't aware of their situation, so if asked directly, they deny any kind of abuse.

"A beating," Andrea says. "You didn't get to eat the next day. You don't get the training we did by being babied."

I nod. Kendall Cooper's parents were abusive, and she tried to run away with her sister. "So what happened on the day of Natalie's death?"

"Well, that's kind of a long story," she says, chuckling.

"I have time," I say, not breaking my expression.

"Well, it was..." Andrea pauses. "Maybe two years ago. Back when I still lived with my parents. It was late at night. Like, almost midnight, and I heard our home alarm system go off. Ma'am and Sir never mentioned that we had one, so it startled the lot of us. I got up out of bed and told the rest of the kids to stay put. I noticed that Natalie and Kendall weren't there, but I didn't think too much of it. When I got downstairs, Ma'am and Sir were already there. I assumed that they were the source of the noise, but they weren't.

"We didn't know what was happening, but Natalie was one of the only kids who knew the passcode to the safe, and sure enough, it was cleared out. The only things in there were our blueprints to Fort Knox." My heart skips a beat. Fort Knox.

"So, Ma'am and Sir armed themselves and began to go out looking for Natalie and Kendall," she continues. "I was the oldest, so I came too. We heard a rustling in the bushes—our house was pretty far out in the woods—and Ma'am and Sir unloaded their magazines into the underbrush. There's no way of saying which one shot her, but I heard a scream. We trekked through the woods for a few minutes before we found Natalie's body. Kendall was gone, and so were the plans for Fort Knox."

I sit there for a moment, absorbing this new information. Kendall Cooper's parents killed her sister. And she was there to watch as it happened. No wonder she's so messed up. Pity for the young girl who I had thought was horrible, whom I had really believed was a monster, floods my emotions. Again, it's like I'm back on the highway. Staring at *my* sister's dead body. Andrea and I sit there in silence for a minute.

"This was the last time you heard from your sister?" I say finally.

"Yeah," she says. "Both of 'em." She lets out a slight chuckle at that. I have to physically bite my tongue to keep myself from saying something that would lose me my job. Natalie was

Andrea's sister, and she is laughing about her death?! The woman is sociopathic! Then a thought crosses my mind. What if Kendall Cooper is too? What if this girl is so broken that she is beyond saving? At least some people can reform in prison, but what if this kid is simply too far gone? What then? Why do I care? Why should I care if Kendall Cooper is a sociopath or just borderline? It's all the same to me. I just need to catch her.

But then comes the thought of Amanda yet again. Kendall Cooper was the person who dragged the body in the morgue—Natalie—away. She tried to save someone she loved and failed. How different is Kendall Cooper from me, really? I don't think I want to know the answer to that question.

Before I dig myself into a metaphorical hole about my moral obligations, I stand up.

"Thank you for your cooperation," I say and walk out of the room.

CHAPTER NINETEEN

KENDALL

The van parks a few blocks away. I know that this will be the last time we see it when we get out. I shove my hands in the pockets of my jacket, pulling the jacket down a little farther than usual so that the bulge of the gun in the holster is less noticeable. Thank god that it's winter, and a cold one at that, so this motion doesn't look in the least bit suspicious. My ski mask is in my pocket. Our plan is to put them on when we're about a block away. There's no need to draw attention to ourselves before the actual robbery starts. Alejandro and I begin the walk to the bank. It should take us about five minutes to get there, but we are supposed to wait for the signal before coming in. We can hide out in a small alleyway next to the building.

The walk to the bank is quiet. Neither of us speaks the whole way. I can't tell if it's because we don't want to draw attention to ourselves or we're not sure if we're still mad at each other. Probably both. But our emotions can't get in the way now. Regardless of how we feel about it, we're on the job now, and our job is to get what we want out of the bank and get everyone back safely.

We make our way into the alley, and it is immediately apparent that it was never meant to be an alleyway. Alejandro can barely fit in sideways. He makes a grunting noise as he slides in after me, careful not to be seen. As uncomfortable and impractical as it may be, hiding in the alleyway is a good strategy. It's small, dark, and no one would expect us to be in here.

"Great hiding spot for us," Alejandro whispers sarcastically. "I'm really enjoying not being able to move."

I put on my ski mask, and he does the same. "If you had a problem with the plan, you could have just not let us go. No use complaining now."

"No," he whispers. "You were right. After Fort Knox, I just wanted to keep us safe. But for people like us, the recognition is as important as the money, if not more."

I know why I need the recognition, but I've always believed that Alejandro and his gang were just in it for the money.

"What do you mean?" I ask, now curious.

"When I crossed the border to America, I was just a teenager," he says. "A few years older than you. And my parents, they were so excited to come. You know when you hear about America, you hear about the promise of a new life, better jobs, wealth. You give up everything just to come here."

"Too bad it's not all that it was talked up to be," I whisper.

"Exactly," he whispers back. "We came here as bottom-of-the-barrel immigrants. We worked the lowest-paying factory jobs. And after work, we were harassed, mugged, by men who got paid better than we did, who didn't have to worry about when their next bill was going to come, or if their families were going to starve the next day." All I can do is nod. Alejandro has never talked about his past before.

"Eduardo, Cecelia, and I," he continues, "we could work just as hard as the white men in this country, and still people would not respect us. The only way we can climb the ranks, the only way people will ever respect us, is if they fear us."

I don't know how to respond to that. No one has ever really talked to me about personal stuff before. Even Natalie had things she would never talk to me about, even if I asked.

The thought of Natalie sharpens my focus. I can't get distracted. I have to remember that I'm doing all of this for her. Not for me. Not for Alejandro. Or Eduardo. Or Cecelia. Or the gang. Natalie.

As if on cue, I hear yelling in the bank, and a single gunshot rings out. That's our signal. Alejandro moves out first, and I follow, getting my gun out of its holster. Alejandro opens the door, and I see Juan and three other gang members each with an automatic rifle pointed at the ceiling. There are half a dozen customers and maybe three or four employees in the main lobby of the bank. I close the door and turn the bolt to lock it. Alejandro and I point our guns at the people, who are beginning to gather into a group.

"Everyone throw your phones down or I'll shoot!" I yell. They all obey and throw their phones in my direction. I put my gun in the holster and stomp on every single one of them. Can't have them calling the police on us. I then walk over to the windows and close all the fancy curtains. The only way people could possibly see us now is through the glass door, which is locked. I walk over behind the desks, which are on the left side of the room from the door. I am not at all surprised to see that the two bank employees are huddled together on the ground, conversing. One of them is a pale man with dark hair who looks like he's in his thirties, and the other is an older woman with silver hair, maybe around sixty years old. The woman has her back turned, and the man is turned toward me. He gasps at the sight of me, and his shaky hand points behind the woman's shoulder. She turns around, and her mouth falls open. Then a mixture of fear and determination appears on her face, and she stands up.

"I've already lived a good, long life," she says defiantly. "And I am going to tell you, young lady, that you are wasting yours." A wave of rage engulfs me. How dare this woman even *think* she is in a position to give me life advice? In one swift motion, I take my gun out of its holster, raise it, and shoot her in the chest. As she falls to the floor, eyes open wide in a stunned expression, I squat down next to her.

"You're wrong," I say so softly only the woman could hear me if she were alive. "Half my life was a waste. I won't make that same mistake again." I hear a clicking sound and see that the man has pressed the button that is supposed to set off the bank alarm. Nothing happens. He presses it again. Nothing happens. I smile and stand up.

"Now that's not going to work," I say in the same tone I used with the old lady. "We hacked the system. Congratulations! By pushing that button, you have now trapped yourselves in this building and cut off power to all your landlines." The man's eyes grow wide as I walk closer to him.

"Please—" he begs, putting his hands up. "Please don't hurt me." What a pussy. I continue to walk toward him, and he whimpers softly. I smile under my mask. So this is how real power feels. When just approaching someone terrifies them to their core. It occurs to me that I relish this feeling.

I slowly kneel down so that I'm on the man's level, and a tear runs down his cheek. I motion toward the group of people in the lobby with my gun.

"Why don't you go join your friends?" He frantically gets up and joins the group of people in the lobby. I turn to Alejandro, and he nods at me. I nod back and begin to make my way to the vault. If everything went according to plan, the rest of the gang should have taken out all the security guards.

When I turn the corner, I see Eduardo and the man with the scar standing outside the vault. I breathe a sigh of relief, because this is proof that the plan went well. The rest of the gang should be stealing our getaway vehicle right about now. Juan is holding three backpacks for the three of us to put our loot in.

"Everything's OK," I say. "You can start on the vault now." We couldn't run the risk of the bank alarm going off, so the plan was for Eduardo to wait until I gave the OK to start hacking the vault. I turn around and walk back to the lobby, where the man at the front desk is still huddled with the other people. I point my gun at him. "You, give me the keys to the deposit boxes."

He hurries over to the counter, and his hand shakes as he fumbles with his lanyard to get the right key out. When he finally does, he uses it to unlock a drawer, which contains boxes of keys, all labeled. There are five, and he pulls them out one by one and begins to stack them on top of each other. He turns and looks at the old lady's body, which is still squirting blood all over the floor, and then back at me. I can feel his emotions rising.

"Go back to where you were," I instruct, slowly, although I can tell he's thinking about resisting, and I back up a little bit, but not enough. I am off balance and far too close to him to react when he launches himself on top of me. I fire a shot, and I think it hit him in the shoulder, but he doesn't seem to notice. The gun flies out of my hand, and I hear it skid across the floor. I can only hope that one of the gang members has enough sense to pick it up. When I land, the man is on top of me, and I buck my hips to offset his center of gravity, sending him toppling. It works, and he falls forward, sticking his arm out to catch himself. I scoot myself out from beneath him and sweep the arm out from under him with my leg. He falls flat on his face, and I take the opportunity to stand up. As he attempts to do the same, I drop a knee on his back, and this time he doesn't get up. I doubt I killed him, but I definitely broke something. I stand up and see Juan with my gun in his hand. He hands it to me. I take it and shoot the man in the leg so he's not tempted to get up again and put up a fight.

I walk over to the counter and pick up the five boxes he stacked for me, then begin my walk to the vault for a second time. I turn the corner and see Eduardo and the man with the scar exactly where they were before.

"Are you almost done?" I ask Eduardo.

"Almost," Eduardo says. He clacks the laptop keys for about a minute before the light on the safe finally turns green, and Eduardo twists the knob. We run in, and I set the boxes of keys down on the floor and take them out one by one. Each key is labeled with a box number, and I realize I'll have to go through every key to unlock each individual box. That will take more than enough time for the police to get here.

"There has to be some kind of master key for these," I say. "Finding every key for every box is going to take way too long."

"I have an idea," Eduardo says. "But I need some time."

"Well, work fast," I say. Eduardo mumbles something about the mainframe, motherboard, all the boxes being connected to one system as he plugs in his laptop and begins to type away like there's no tomorrow, which there won't be if he doesn't get this done in time. I guard the door as he hacks away. After about five minutes, I'm getting impatient. It feels as if the police are about to storm the building any minute.

Just as I'm about to suggest that getting the boxes unlocked one by one would be quicker, Eduardo yells, "I got it!" and every box door swings open.

"Get everything in!" I say. "Quickly!" I grab a backpack and begin to slide everything from the first deposit box I see. There must be at least a hundred boxes in here, but with the three of us working together, we're done in less than two minutes. We may have broken some of the expensive jewelry, but the fragments will still sell. I hand my backpack to Eduardo.

"Get out now! I'll get the others!" I say, running to the front lobby and see a customer outside who seems to be getting frus-trated with the locked door. She's trying to get in. She looks up and sees me in the mask. She gapes at me and backs away.

She begins to run away. Well, shit. The cops will be here within minutes.

I run over to where the gang is keeping the hostages. "Come on!" I yell. "We're leaving!" They all sling their weapons on their shoulders and follow me out the back. When we finally get to the back parking lot, a man I recognize from the hideout this morning is there waiting for us in another stolen vehicle. This time it's a black minivan. Classy. I dive into a seat, and once I'm sure everyone else is in, I close the door. We speed away.

CHAPTER TWENTY

DANIELLE

As I drive home, my head pounds. It reminds me of a time as a kid when I had been climbing a tree and fell, hitting my head. The only thing that makes this worse is that when I fell, my sister helped me up and called my parents to take care of me. My sister isn't here anymore.

Is that why I cared so much about the girl today? Kendall Cooper? Is that why, when I heard about what happened to her, I was so worried that she was beyond saving? Because I know what she's going through? Because I lost my sister? But Kendall Cooper is more than just some criminal. She's a person. If any-thing, today was proof of that. She had a life. She had a family. She *lost* that family. No wonder she snapped. She wants to make other people hurt the way she's hurting. Or maybe she just needs to take her anger out on something. Maybe both. I don't know. I really shouldn't care.

But that doesn't mean we're alike. Even if Kendall Cooper warrants some measure of sympathy, I certainly don't. She was trying to help her sister. I got mine killed. I made a mistake, and my sister paid the price. She and I are nothing alike. So why am I so upset over her? I don't know.

When I finally turn into the driveway, all I do know is that I need a drink and a nap. But of course, I can't, because as soon as I get home, Jason is in the kitchen waiting for me. He of all people will know that something is wrong, and being the lovely husband that he is, he will try to get me to talk about it. God, he can be so annoyingly perfect sometimes.

When I walk into the kitchen, Jason has two glasses of wine ready.

"Hey, honey," he says. When I give no response, he sets the wine glasses down and frowns. "Long day?"

"Like you wouldn't believe," I say. My eyes wander to the glass of wine on Jason's right. "I could use that drink right about now." Jason picks up the glass and holds it out to me. "All yours," he says. I take it from him and take a huge gulp. The alcohol dims my emotions a bit, and Jason's eyes glint with concern. "What happened?"

"You know the girl I told you about," I begin. "The one who broke into Fort Knox?"

"Yeah," he says.

"Turns out she has a name," I say. "Kendall Cooper. She was part of some elite crime organization. The Mors Clan."

"Was?" he asks. "You mean she left? The crimes she committed seem like they were too organized for a kid to come up with on her own."

"No," I continue. "I spoke to her sister today in the Arkansas State Prison. Well, one of her sisters, anyway. She said she was smart. Smarter than anyone else in the family. Her mother trained them."

"Whoa, whoa, slow down," he says, holding his hand up. He walks around the counter and stops beside me. "So this family was a big part of this organization."

"Yeah," I say. "Apparently, they had a lot of kids. They would train the kids for big jobs, like Fort Knox. Her sister said Kendall was among the best."

"What happened?" he asks. "How did she get out?"

"She ran away," I say. "Two years ago, with one of her sisters. The woman I interviewed, Andrea, said that Kendall was close with her sister Natalie, and they ran away together. Kendall made it out, but Natalie didn't. I saw the body." I want to kick myself for the choking feeling in my throat when I mention the death of Kendall's sister. I loathe myself.

"Oh my god," he said and pauses. "So how did she end up at Fort Knox and all?"

"When she and her sister ran away two years ago," I say, "they stole the unfinished plans to break into Fort Knox. How Kendall teamed up with the people that did the job with her, I don't know."

"Wow," Jason says. "That's a lot."

All of a sudden, I have the urge to cry. I swallow it, willing myself not to break down. Just then, both our phones buzz at the same time. That means that it's the station. We both chuckle a bit and pull away. I pick up my phone and see a text from the chief.

Full day tomorrow, it says.

I don't really know whether to laugh or cry when I read that. I just want this case to be over. I just want to put Cooper behind bars and call it a night.

"Oh my god," Jason says. He looks up at me, and I can tell by the expression on his face that it's important.

"What is it?" I ask.

"There was a robbery at the State Reserve Bank," he says. "The message says that a suspect of interest to you may have been involved."

"Oh no," I say. "You don't think it was—"

"Kendall Cooper?" he finishes. "Most likely." He walks over to the coat rack by the front door and begins to put his jacket on. "I have to go."

I sigh. "We just can't catch a break lately."

CHAPTER TWENTY-ONE

KENDALL

I sit in the back of the van. Because we may have been recognized from Fort Knox, everyone who went on that job is in the back, and one of the new guys is driving. I hope he knows what he's doing. What if we get pulled over? Who knows how much experience this guy has? He could give us away. What if this was his first job? I'm so stupid for letting these new guys help; they're only making things more complicated.

Sitting on either side of me are Alejandro and Juan, and aside from the occasional rumble from the van, suggesting that it is in need of a tune-up, the ride is completely silent. We've been driving for about an hour and a half when we stop. I assume that means we're at one of the gang's hideouts. There are three, but the dugout is the main one. That's where we are.

The back doors to the van open, and sunlight shines in, forcing me to squint. I see Juan hop outside, motioning for us to come out. We all keep our gloves and face coverings on so that we don't get any fingerprints or DNA on the evidence we are about to drop off here. Since we have practically an unlimited supply of money, we can get rid of these guns tomorrow and buy new ones for our next job. Despite the lack of news reports, I've decided that breaking into Fort Knox was the right move. If nothing else, it got the government's attention, and it gave us some spending money for future jobs.

I get out of the van to see that Juan is there waiting for me. I bump into him and, annoyed, shove him out of the way.

"Move," I say. "You smell like shit."

"What is your deal?" He throws his hands up in frustration.

"You're useless," I mutter. I don't have the energy for this.

"Why do you get so mad over shit like this?" he exclaims. "Just calm the fuck down! I'm not the one trying to arrest you, remember?" I roll my eyes so far, I can nearly see my brain. There are no witnesses here, right? I could just kill him. Though I doubt Alejandro would appreciate it.

"I'm the reason you're rich, remember?" I retort. "Don't get your drunk ass all twisted in a knot now." I turn around and start to walk away.

"You have allies, Kendall," Juan calls after me. I stop but don't turn to look at him. "You do know that not everyone is your enemy, don't you?" The question catches me off guard, and I turn to look at Juan.

"It's not my fault half of the gang is incompetent," I say, walking toward him. "Including you. You're not an ally, Juan. You're a tool."

I expect him to defend himself or his competence in the gang, but instead Juan looks at me with these strange, sad eyes.

"I knew someone like you once," he said.

"What?" I ask. Juan looks around, as if an unseen person were listening.

"I had a kid once, you know. A son," he says. For some reason, that makes me mad. I don't care about Juan's damn kid. I don't have time for him; I don't have time for this.

That's what I should have said. But instead, I say, "Where is he?" I bite my tongue, willing no other unwarranted words to escape my lips.

"If I knew, I would tell you," he says, then locks eyes with me. "He was like you." I don't know what to say to that, so I just keep staring at Juan. "He thought he had to do everything alone."

At that, I recover myself and shake my head sternly. "I don't know your kid, but don't get us mixed up," I say, my voice not nearly as strong as I would like it to be. I try for an assertive tone once more. "You would never understand." My voice sounds young, almost weak. I feel myself beginning to fume. "This is such bullshit! The fuck do you want, Juan?"

"I want you to understand," he says. "He ran away because he felt like he had nothing. He was dealing with his own problems, and it was my fault that I couldn't help him." I don't say anything. "I know you don't know me very well, but let me help you."

Where the fuck did this come from? Juan's a drunk; he's practically useless. Why would he ever want to help me?

"If I needed your help, I would ask for it," I say. "Now, if you speak again before I clean this gun, I will shoot you with it." I storm off before he can say anything else. I don't want to understand Juan. I don't care about his son. I don't care about him. I just want to complete my goal, whether he is a part of it or not. But something about that conversation with him was different. Juan has never spoken to me like that before, or anyone in the gang for that matter. It almost seemed like he actually...trusted me. Go fucking figure. Maybe Juan is different than I assumed he was. Maybe he's someone who really would help me.

CHAPTER TWENTY-TWO

DANIELLE

Thirteen injured or dead guards. Two dead lobby workers. Half a dozen scared witnesses. Kendall Cooper, what did you do now?

If I had my suspicions that it was Cooper before I came, they are confirmed without a doubt when I spot Agent Danvers as soon as I arrive.

I walk over to her and the three other FBI agents that she's talking to. When I'm within earshot, she waves them away, and they split off to do their various assigned tasks.

"Detective Toole," she says, with her hands behind her back. "Good to see you again."

"And you, Agent Danvers," I say. "We've been seeing quite a lot of each other lately."

"Yes," Agent Danvers says. "I wish it could be under better circumstances, but I have information for you."

"What is it?" I ask.

"My agents and I have spoken to witnesses at the bank, and their descriptions of the suspects were similar to the ones from Fort Knox," she says.

"And the girl?" I ask, lowering my voice.

"I'm afraid so," Agent Danvers says, matching my tone. "Several witnesses said there was a young woman with them. Many of them guessed late teens to early twenties, but she had a mask on. Some of my agents analyzed her voice and cross-referenced it with the footage from the Fort. It's definitely our girl."

I nod. "What do you need me to do?"

"Well, your partner is interviewing the last of the witnesses," Agent Danvers says. "I suggest you go join her, but I need one more thing from you."

"What?" I ask.

"A name," she says. I know she's talking about Cooper.

"Kendall Cooper," I say. "I interviewed her sister just yesterday."

"Kendall Cooper," she repeats. "Thank you." She walks away.

~

I find Nicki in the back parking lot, where a team of forensic investigators are collecting evidence. Nicki is interviewing a witness, and I wait until the witness walks away to approach her. She smiles when she sees me.

"Good to see you up and around again," I say.

"Good to be back," she replies. "Looks like the kid strikes again."

"Yeah, no shit," I say grimly. "Not with a lot of mercy, either."

"Yup," Nicki says, with no hint of sympathy in her voice. "That's our kid for you. Several witnesses placed her. I interviewed them myself. Said it was brutal. Killed two employees, one a senior citizen. You can't tell me that the old lady was a threat to her. She must have killed just for the thrill of it."

I nod, and the same feeling from last night arises inside me. A mix of pity for this girl and horror at what she has done overwhelms me. But I can't think of this particular incident emotionally. I need to be logical. After Fort Knox, why come back out into the open? It only gives the police a higher chance of finding her, and it's not like she was in need of the money. Maybe Nicki is right. Maybe Kendall Cooper is far beyond saving, and she just enjoys the thrill of the kill. I hate that this information presents itself to me as a fact, instead of just some notion. I can't shake the feeling that some part buried deep inside of me actually...cares for her. Actually cares if she's worth saving. And that terrifies me.

"What is it?" she asks.

"It just doesn't make sense," I say. "I mean, tactically, this group of people, including the kid, were so clever in breaking into Fort Knox. They found weaknesses, disguised themselves as guards, penetrated the building, and made themselves rich like it was just another Tuesday. It feels so...out of character for them to then do something so rash and seemingly pointless. I mean, they have to know that they should stay in hiding after pulling a stunt like that."

"Well, they did take more precautions than last time," Nicki says. "For starters, they wore ski masks."

I nod, wondering why they hadn't been wearing masks during the Fort Knox heist. Why the change of heart? "I interviewed the second DNA match."

Nicki's face lights up. "How was it? Did you get anything out of her?"

I tell her everything—about Andrea, Kendall, Natalie, their family—and when I'm done, Nicki's expression darkens. There is a minute of silence between us.

"That's rough," she says finally. "She was part of the Mors Clan, for god's sake! We need to catch her before she does any more damage."

I feel another swell of emotion at the thought of putting Kendall Cooper behind bars, but I nod anyway. "Agreed. But what's our plan? We haven't gotten any more information from the bank robbery than what we already know."

"I have no idea," she says. "This was a clean and quick robbery; it took no more than ten to fifteen minutes. There is nearly no evidence left behind at the scene."

"Well then, what are our options?" I ask. "Like I said, this attack doesn't make strategic sense, so if this is her last crime before she goes back into hiding, it might also be our last evidence before the case goes cold."

"You're right, but there is one other option. I've been thinking about it a lot."

"What's that?" I ask.

"In the past, civilian aid has been a big help in solving cases. Social media has made it nearly impossible to stay under the radar these days. If we can't catch her using forensics, our best chance at finding her is for someone to spot her."

"So what you're saying is—" I begin.

"We make information about Kendall Cooper public," Nicki finishes.

~

"Why is it that whenever you two come to me, you are trying to convince me to do something for you?" Agent Danvers asks, clearly annoyed at Nicki and me.

"This isn't just for us," Nicki says. "This will help your investigation too."

"We can't risk the public finding out about her," Agent Danvers says, dismissing the request entirely. "Imagine how that would make the U.S. government look. You two aren't thinking about the consequences. It would make us look incompetent, a laughing stock to our allies in other countries. Our crime levels could spike. The possibilities are endless if we release this to the media."

"But Kendall Cooper and whoever she's working with have the potential to do a lot of damage. Maybe more harm than any other criminals in this country," I say. "They're organized and dangerous, and they may not be planning on stopping. I mean, look around: We haven't found any more information about them than we already had. They're good at covering their tracks. If we don't do this, there might be no chance at stopping them."

Agent Danvers seems to be considering it, and after a moment, she speaks. "You may be right, but even if you are, I would have to run the order up the chain of command. I may outrank the two of you, but I certainly cannot present this information to the public on my own authority."

"Then run it up the chain," Nicki says. "Persuade whoever you need to. Please, it could help a lot if you would just try."

Agent Danvers sighs. "I suppose I could arrange a meeting with the head of the FBI, but even if I can, I'll make no promises."

I know this is all she can do. "Thank you," I say.

CHAPTER TWENTY-THREE

KENDALL

We clean our guns and dispose of them, and by the time we get home, it's the next day. When we hop out of the van, Cecelia and Milo are already out front waiting for us. I hope Cecelia cooked, because the three of us haven't eaten since lunch before the job. And while I can handle hunger, Eduardo has been complaining the entire time about how hungry he is. Why is he such a god-damn child?

Cecelia beams when she sees us, and when the van stops, she immediately walks up to Alejandro. He gives her a kiss on the cheek and says something in Spanish that I don't quite catch. I think he might be apologizing for being gone so long. Eduardo doesn't acknowledge either of them and instead walks inside.

Milo runs up to me, and I give him a good ear scratch. I can tell he missed me. I try to distract myself by petting him while Alejandro and Cecelia engage in a long kiss. I've never been one for romantic affection.

I let myself inside and see that Cecelia has indeed cooked for us. Only now, once I smell the food, do I let myself feel my hunger. That's how I would get by when Sir and Ma'am punished me: I would refuse to feel anything until the punishment was over. However, I have discipline, and since Alejandro and Cecelia aren't back yet, I go to my room to get cleaned up. I change out of my dirty, bloody clothes, change into clean ones and throw them in the washing machine. Until they are clean, those clothes are evidence, and if someone were to come to the house, I wouldn't want the clothes to be found. They have to be washed or discarded immediately. I turn on the washing machine then grab my hairbrush, and head into the bathroom. As I look at my reflection in the mirror, a memory floods my mind, and I can't think of anything else.

I'm nine. It's the night after my first kill. I look in the mirror and wipe the tears off my face. Ma'am was right. I am weak. I am a pathetic, stupid child who doesn't understand the bigger picture. If I don't fall in line soon, Ma'am and Sir will have no use for me, and they'll discard me like I never existed. If I want to survive, if I want to be a part of the Mors Clan, I have to fight.

I begin to clean myself up in preparation for bed, but I can't focus. Even my reflection looks different. When I look in the mirror, I don't see myself anymore. I see a killer. A murderer. I hate it. I decide to go to bed without washing myself. Sitting on my bed is Natalie. We share a room, since we're so close in age. I sit down on our little mattress on the floor. It's not ideal, but when you move around as much as we do, you can't expect ideal. I sit down on the bed next to Natalie. Neither of us says anything.

She puts her arm around my shoulders, and I rest my head against her.

"You did the right thing," she says, finally breaking the silence.

"It doesn't feel like it," I confess. Natalie is the only person I can confide my feelings to. If I said that to anyone else in my family, it would end in a beating.

"The first kill is always the hardest," she says. "It gets better, I promise."

"How?" I ask. "How could killing people possibly get easier?" I realize my voice is rising, and Natalie shushes me. I look up at her, and she appears deep in thought. I know she is haunted by her own memories of killings. Even though she tries to hide them from me, I know Natalie has her own demons.

"I don't know," she says finally. "Our lives shouldn't be this way, but they are. Whether we like it or not, this is what we have to do to survive."

I didn't know it back then, but that day Natalie had unknowingly planted the seed that would blossom into the idea that we could change our lives. The idea that we could run away and control our own futures. The idea that would get Natalie killed.

I set down the hairbrush and go into the kitchen to join Eduardo, Cecelia, and Alejandro. Cecelia is setting the table, and I begin to help her before she even asks. I need something else to occupy my mind, to keep me from breaking down and starting to throw things. I grab the plates and begin setting them out. I distract myself by counting out the different pieces of silverware. One. Two. Three. Four. Plates. One. Two. Three. Four. Forks. One. Two. Three. Four. Spoons.

By the time the table is set, I feel a little better. Well, better enough not to throw anything. Cecelia encourages us to dig in while glaring at Eduardo, since he clearly already felt free to. He doesn't seem to notice. I try to be polite and take small bites, but once I begin to eat Cecelia's delicious food, I can't help but eat more. I notice Alejandro doing the same; he clearly doesn't know you're supposed to pause between helpings. If you eat too much, too quickly when you're starving, your stomach can't handle it and you throw up. I tell him this, and he slows down a bit, but not much. I know he can't help it. He's not as used to being hungry as I am. But even my discipline is wavering, because in the past when I've been starving, the food has never been nearly this good.

After I finish eating what I think is my normal meal size, I put my plate in the sink and begin to scrub it. I'm still hungry, but I don't want to overeat. I help Cecelia clean up and put the remaining food in the fridge before grabbing Milo's food bowl and going to my room. I scoop some food into his bowl and set it down. He begins to munch on it, but I can't help but wonder if Cecelia gave him better food while I was gone. She sometimes gives him leftovers when she cooks, and if it was just her, I'd imagine there were a lot of those. He probably hates when I come back to only ever feed him dog kibble. Something about the image of Cecelia feeding him leftover chicken scraps lightens my mood a bit.

After he's done, I take him out the front door to do his business. In the time we've been inside, the sun has begun to rise, and streaks of pink and orange stain the morning sky. The woods are beginning to chirp, shuffle, and rustle to life. I sit on the front steps as Milo sniffs around the woods, looking for a place to do his business.

It's only now that I can finally be alone with my thoughts. My mind drifts to Juan and our conversation yesterday morning. It was odd, to say the least. I don't think anyone outside of the people who live with me really trusts me. You can't really trust when you live like this. But Juan...he seemed to genuinely trust me with the information he was giving. That's what threw me off, and yet I don't know if *I* trust him. I've never known him to be a great con man or a supreme liar, but I don't really know him. Alejandro trusts him, and I guess that was always enough for me to let him in on our plans. But now he's offering more. I just need to decide: If the time comes when I need his help, would I accept his offer?

Before I can think about it any more, I hear Alejandro calling me inside.

I come inside and see him and Cecelia sitting on the couch. Milo follows me, and I close the door. "What is it?" I ask.

Alejandro points to the TV. "Cecelia and I have been watching the local news," he says. "Nothing about the bank robbery. Not a single mention of it."

"What?!" I exclaim. My voice is calm, but I can almost taste the venom in my mouth. I storm over to the junk room and kick Eduardo off the computer so I can boot up a search. He protests that he was working and has a quick roll call with every curse word in the book, but I ignore him.

I type in the name of the bank and hit the plus sign, then type in "robbery." There are only about a dozen news reports on it, and the details are minimal. I can feel the blood rushing to my face. I pound my fist against the top of the desk then storm back over to the TV.

"There's almost nothing," I say. "They're covering it up. Again." I feel panic rising in my chest. This isn't working. Nothing's working! I have tried twice to push my plan forward, to ruin Ma'am and Sir, to fix what has happened, but the damn government is derailing everything.

Alejandro stands up. "What should we do?"

"We need to find another job," I reply without hesitation. "It's the only way."

CHAPTER TWENTY-FOUR

DANIELLE

I grab a cup of coffee and walk back to my desk. I'm at the point in the case where I'm stuck. Only it's worse this time, because this is technically the FBI's case, and I have limited resources because everything is classified. So not only do I have no leads, but even if I did, I don't know if I would be able to do anything about it unless I got a call from Agent Danvers giving me the OK.

This whole situation annoys me, but I have to remember that I am doing this to catch Kendall Cooper. No one will understand her or be able to reason with her the way I can. Still, the thought of using my empathy for her to sway her in an interrogation rubs me the wrong way. The image of Cooper behind bars makes me sick to my stomach.

Some people reform in prison. Maybe I could get her into therapy or a support group or something. It sounds so stupid. I don't even know this girl, and I'm already making plans to help her.

I repeat the thought in my head. *Help her.* What the hell am I doing here? Just because I can empathize with this kid doesn't change the fact that she is a killer. It doesn't matter if I know what she went through or not. What matters is that she is a criminal. Thoughts like that are going to lose me the job I spent years working my ass off for. But still, the image of Cooper's face behind bars remains fixed in my mind.

Nicki walks over to my desk. "I'm guessing you're not getting anywhere either?" I say.

She sighs. "Nope. Any ideas?"

"No," I say. "We don't even know if Agent Danvers is going to be able to get the suspect's information out, so there's pretty much nothing we can do now."

"What about psychological profiling?" Nicki suggests, sitting at her desk as she rummages through old case files.

"Psychological profiling," I repeat.

"It's a method used for suspect identification based on crime scene evidence," she says. "In our case, we can use it to figure out if Cooper will turn up again, or where she might be hiding."

"We've never done it before," I say. "It seems like a bit of a stretch."

"If you have any other ideas, I'm all ears," she says. "But you said it yourself: We're not getting anywhere right now."

I consider it. We do need all the help we can get. Plus, if I'm able to understand Cooper better, maybe I'll be able to figure out what exactly I'm feeling in regard to her situation.

"OK," I say. "Let's do it."

~

Thank god it was Agent Danvers who called and not me. I can only imagine how that conversation would go. Even though she's the one who put us on the case, I don't think she likes us badgering her about it every other day. She seems annoyed whenever we talk to her.

I pick up the phone. "Hello?"

"Detective Toole," Agent Danvers says. "I just wanted to let you and your partner know that I did my personal best to convince the head of the FBI to make the information about our suspect public. It's out of my hands now."

"Thank you," I say. "That's all we can ask for. But I actually have a question for you."

"Yes?" she says.

"Since we have no further leads on the suspect, we were hoping to get her psychologically profiled in order to get more information about her," I say. "I wanted to run that by you and see if you could recommend anyone, since this is classified."

"Psychologically profiled?" Agent Danvers says. "Give me a minute." I hear her set down the phone and the clacking of a keyboard on the other end. After about a minute, she picks up the phone again. "There's a guy that works for us about half an hour from your station. I'll email you the address." Like magic, an email from Agent Danvers sails into my inbox.

"Thank you," I say. I hang up.

"See?" Nicki teases. "Agent Danvers didn't think it was such a bad idea."

"Shut up," I say, opening the email she sent me. I put the address in my directions. "Let's go."

~

Like Agent Danvers said, the drive is about thirty minutes. We turn the radio on to listen to the national news, since both of us have communication devices on in case the station needs to contact us.

"Breaking news just in from national law enforcement: A physical description and a name of a suspect from last month's Fort Knox break-in has been released."

Nicki and I look at each other in shock. Agent Danvers did it. Nicki reaches over and turns the radio up.

"One of the suspects in the break-in has now been identified. The name of the suspect is Kendall Cooper, and she is a *minor*." The news reporter pauses for a moment, as if for effect, but I wonder if it is her that is in shock. "Law enforcement describe Ms. Cooper as a Caucasian female between the ages of thirteen and eighteen, with dirty blonde hair, hazel eyes, approximately 5'4", and likely in the Tennessee, Kentucky area. She was last spotted wearing black leggings and a black zip-up sweatshirt. If you see anyone matching this description, please call your local law enforcement." She moves on, talking about a surge in harsh weather in the south, but Nicki turns the radio off.

"She did it," Nicki says after a long silence. "I mean, I didn't think that it would actually work. Do you think this could help our investigation?"

"That's why we did it, right?" I say. "We need to get this kid, Nicki, and we have to do whatever we need to do that."

"Yeah," she agrees. "It's crazy how big this is. This is the biggest case you and I have ever done together. Those old break-ins and homicides are going to seem boring after this." I pull out the picture of Kendall Cooper from my folder and stare at it absentmindedly.

"Yeah," I say quietly.

"If you don't want to talk right now, that's fine," Nicki says, her tone significantly more serious.

"What do you mean?" I ask, putting the image back in the case file.

"We're heading onto 465," she says. I don't say anything for a moment. I try to think about where we're going. About the case. I can't think about where we are. I can't open the floodgates to what happened here.

I clear my throat. "No, it's fine. We can keep talking. I don't care." Even after I say this, silence still hangs in the air between us.

"You know that if you ever need to talk about it, I'm here for you. Right?" Nicki says.

"Yeah," I say in a voice that sounds entirely unlike my own. "Yeah, of course I know that. But you don't need to worry about me. I'm fine."

Neither of us speaks much for the rest of the car ride. We pull into the parking lot of the address Agent Danvers gave me. We are the only ones here, and I'm not sure if that's a good or bad thing.

When we walk in, there is a man at the front desk, typing away on a computer. He barely acknowledges us.

"Excuse me, sir," Nicki says. The man looks up in surprise, as if he has only just noticed that we are there, which is probably an accurate statement. He straightens up and adjusts his glasses.

"What can I do for you?" he asks.

"We were sent by Agent Danvers," I say. "I assume she informed you that we were coming?"

"Oh yes!" he says and points to a gray door to the right of his desk. "He's right in there." I'm not exactly sure who "he" is, but I can only assume that he's the profiler. Nicki walks in first, and I follow her. A man of about sixty years old is taking notes on a notepad with his back turned to us. He is sitting at a desk that looks as old as he is.

"Hello?" Nicki asks. Unlike the man at the front desk, this man doesn't even flinch when he hears us.

"Hello, detectives," he says without turning around. "My apologies, I'll be with you in just a moment." He scribbles down a few more words, then turns his chair to face us. "So, you have a suspect for me?" I'm assuming Agent Danvers contacted him as well.

"Yes," I say, opening my notebook. "Kendall Cooper."

"The girl that was on the news," he says slowly, as if thinking hard about each syllable. "Interesting. You two are on the investigation?" He sounds doubtful but maintains his composure.

"Yes," Nicki says but doesn't give him any more information than that. He just nods and boots up his computer. Once the screen lights up, he opens a document and begins to ask us questions.

"What crimes do you know that the suspect has committed?" he asks.

"She was born into a crime organization," I say. "The Mors Clan. It's relatively well known around the Southeast. There are likely far more than we are aware of, but the ones we know about are the Nashville bombing, the robbery of Fort Knox, and the robbery of the State Reserve Bank."

He types the information into the document. "She was born into a crime organization," he says. "Any known trauma?"

"Her parents taught her and her siblings the ways of crime, but they were highly abusive. Failing an assignment or doing poorly in training would result in starvation or a beating, according to Andrea Cooper, her sister," I say. "However, when she and another of her sisters tried to run away, that sister was killed. They were close." My voice is steady and calm, as if I am reciting from a textbook and couldn't care less about what I am saying. I wish that was the case.

"So what you're saying is, lots of trauma," he says, typing steadily. "Estimated age?"

"Thirteen to eighteen," Nicki says. The man types again.

"How far apart were these crimes?" he asks. "The known ones."

"All within the last two months," Nicki says. "The last one was two days ago."

We continue to answer questions about Cooper from the experiences we know she's had, the way she goes about her criminal activities, and the people she has interacted with, drawing on the security footage of her crimes.

After two hours of this, the man finally says, "She's going to strike again soon. And when I say soon, I mean in the next couple of days. She's an impulsive teenager radicalized by her abusive parents and her sister's death; she isn't going to sit around and think hard about her next move. There is a clear pattern here: The Fort Knox break-in occurred two years after she stole the plans, meaning it took patience and calculation. However, soon after this, instead of exhibiting the proper precautions and hiding out, she attacked once more, less than a month after the first attack. Unless you catch her, her attacks will only become more frequent and sloppy."

"Can you make any guesses about where she will strike next?" I ask. He scrolls through the profile he's created.

"Somewhere familiar," he says. "She will likely want to spend as little time as possible planning her next strike. Maybe even somewhere she's struck before. Is there anywhere you can think of where she could cause the most damage?"

I think and almost say no when all of a sudden, it comes to me. I remember how precisely the van was placed, in front of the crowded nightclub. I knew right then that the person who had placed it there wanted to take out as many people as possible.

"I know where she's going to go," I say, making eye contact with Nicki. "We need to contact the station; she's going to the nightclub."

CHAPTER TWENTY-FIVE

KENDALL

"Hold still, honey," Cecelia says. I scrunch my face up and feel a strong urge to squirm, but I hold still. "OK, now look up." I hate this, but I do as she says, and she smears the sticky mascara onto my eyelashes. The only thing preventing me from punching her is reminding myself that this is Cecelia and not someone who is actually trying to kill me. I make a mental note not to mention mascara to the police if I ever get caught. If they used it on me as a torture method, I'd sing like a canary.

"I hate makeup," I decide out loud. Cecelia laughs.

"I did too when I was your age," she says. "But it works on the boys, if you know what I mean." She winks at me, and I chuckle. "OK, now close your eyes." I do, and she sweeps a brush across my eyelids with some sort of powder on it. I assume it's eyeshadow. It's more tolerable than the mascara but still not comfortable on my face.

"Ten minutes!" Alejandro calls from the kitchen.

My eyes are still closed, but I can hear Cecelia's tone change. "So what's the plan for tonight?" she asks. She sounds more serious than I've ever heard her, and her tone is almost concerned.

"Just raiding a bar," I say casually, like it's something we do every day. "Nothing difficult compared to Fort Knox." This job is an attention grab for the press and police. Something we failed spectacularly at with our previous jobs, especially Fort Knox. I need press coverage. If this doesn't work, I have no idea what else I can do. I feel an awful voice in my head beginning to nag at me. *What if I truly can't beat Ma'am and Sir at their own game?* I push the voice away. I will. My plan will work. I just have to do this one more job, and the news outlets won't be able to talk about anything but me. I hear her set the brush down and pick something else up.

"Keep your eyes closed," she says, and I listen.

"What has been your opinion?" I ask, out of the blue. "You know, on the jobs we've done." I realize I've never really asked her how she feels about them. While she's never directly opposed them, she's never really expressed her opinion either.

Cecelia sighs, and I feel a thinner, stickier brush sweep across where my eyelashes meet the lid of my eye. "It's important to you, and to Alejandro..." She trails off. "I just worry. That's all."

"I'll protect the boys," I say. "I promise."

"It's not just them I'm worried about," she says.

I smile. It's sweet to know that she cares that much. She stops applying the sticky eyeshadow, and I open my eyes.

"I can handle myself," I reassure her.

She nods but doesn't seem any less worried.

"You're all done."

She begins to pack up her tote bag full of makeup, and I walk over to the bathroom. I'm wearing a pair of clip in earring, black ripped jeans, black boots, a cropped white t-shirt that exposes my stomach, and a leather jacket over it. The outfit and overall look is supposed to make me appear older. I peer at my reflection in the mirror. I look like a completely different person. I've never really had the luxury of worrying about my appearance, much less the time and effort to attempt to touch it up, but for the first time in my life, I look pretty. I look like someone...desirable. I can't believe that it's me staring back at myself in the mirror.

I catch Alejandro and Eduardo in the kitchen from the reflection in the mirror. I can see them looking at me. I feel a flush of embarrassment come over me and turn away from my reflection to face them.

"Let's go," I say.

~

I sit in the back of the van. Gun in hand. Ready for this. I am so sick of not getting credit for the things I've done. I've been at this, trying to avenge Natalie, for the past two years. I have done the work, and the United States government has ruined it again and again. Well, I'll show them. I'll bomb the fucking White House if that's what it takes to get their attention. If that's what it takes to ruin my parents.

Because of the heightened suspicion and the fact that law enforcement is more likely to recognize us now, we are going to have to make a rolling stop: We will have to actually jump out of the back of the van while it's moving so that no one can see the license plate. The driver and the passenger—both new members of the gang whose names I don't know—are going to use our usual strategy of ditching this van and stealing a new one. That makes us hard to trace.

"Making the jump!" the passenger yells. I make eye contact with Alejandro, and he gives me a firm nod. "In five!" I put my gun in its holster. "Four!" I bend my knees in anticipation. "Three! Two! Now! Go!" Juan throws the back doors of the van open, and we all jump out, except for one member of the gang, who closes the doors.

I try to land on my feet but end up on my knees, skidding across the road. I roll onto my feet and stand up. I look at the rest of the gang, mainly worried about Alejandro and Juan, as they are most integral to our operation. They are both standing up and seem fine. I breathe an internal sigh of relief and motion for us to go into the nightclub, which is booming with the sound of music and people. More people means more victims. More victims will be harder to cover up. That means that, unlike our bigger jobs, our victims won't be a bunch of government operatives willing to keep their near-death experiences or the loss of their loved ones quiet. I scan the perimeter and see no signs of any cops or law enforcement. Good.

We begin to walk around to the line of people on the other side of the building. All our weapons are holstered and concealed underneath a t-shirt or some other item of clothing. When we get in line, no one suspects anything. There must be almost one hundred people waiting in line and even more inside the club. I can still see the ruins of the building across the street. The one that I bombed. How long ago was that? A few weeks? A month? It feels like years. How could I have been so naive? Thinking that the government wouldn't try to cover us up. Cover *me* up. I wonder how long they'll be able to do it. Assuming this goes according to plan, not much longer.

The plan is to wait until we get inside and into the most crowded part of the club before we begin the raid. There's barely any profit from it. We'll steal some money from the bartender, maybe hustle some people for jewelry, but there won't be a whole lot of money in this job. Just damage and death. Just recognition. That's all we really need at this point. We have to wait until we get inside, because for one thing there are more people inside, and two, it's harder to run away from someone with a gun if you are trapped in a confined space.

After what feels like hours, we reach the front of the line. We have our fake IDs ready. If anyone asks tonight, I'm Gabriella Greene. I'm twenty-one years old, and I've lived in Tennessee my whole life. The bouncer is a man of about thirty, skinny, with red hair. He wears a black uniform and has a badge, but something feels off about him. He seems too...easy. There are dozens of people waiting in this line, and they could simply run him over to get inside. Whenever Alejandro and Eduardo would tell stories about coming to this place, they said that it had about half a dozen bouncers inside and at least two at the entrance. I try to re-assure myself that there are a number of reasons why this could be, but something about this is off.

The bouncer scans our IDs and lets us in. I take this as a good sign, because if there was something amiss, the bouncer likely wouldn't have let us in. *Stop being so paranoid,* I tell myself. *The bombing decreased the popularity of the club, so they don't need as many bouncers. Or they're just short staffed. There are myriad different reasons why there is one less bouncer than normal. It isn't enough to cause suspicion.* Even so, the feeling of uneasiness doesn't leave me as I walk in the door.

When we get inside, it's like a flood of drunken people. My home was flooded once, when I was about five or six, and that's the only way to describe this place: a flood. A mess. Bodies on bodies, people dancing, drinking, vomiting. I can barely take a step without bumping into at least three people. The music is so loud I can feel the vibrations through the floor, not to mention the added noise of people talking and singing along. Colored lights flash everywhere, and I realize that if I'm going to be heard, or even noticed, I'm going to need to unplug the sound system. Juan is a couple people away from me, and I motion for him to meet me at the bar. We push through crowds of people before we make it and sit on two stools next to each other. The bartender looks at us expectantly, and Juan grins at him.

"We'd like to open up a tab please," he says politely, and the bartender walks over to the back. He then turns to me. "OK, so what is it?"

"This place is louder than I thought," I say. "I need you to un-plug the music, or shut off the speakers or something, or no one is going to hear us. I'd rather not waste bullets on getting people's attention."

Juan nods. "I've been here before. I know where the main sound system is. I can try to shut it down."

"Good. Take Eduardo with you," I say and watch as he walks away. I know Alejandro and the rest of the gang are stationed around the club, waiting for my signal. I decide to stay by the bar.

"You gonna drink that?" the bartender asks, gesturing to the shot glass. I can't be drunk on a job, but I don't want to seem suspicious, so I nod and pretend to drink it while spilling it over my shoulder. With the black fabric of my jacket and the flashing, colorful lights, I'm almost sure the bartender didn't notice the spill. I set it back down on the counter, and the bartender takes it away. I notice how, the entire time he is working, he doesn't take his eyes off of me. This makes me uneasy. First the bouncer, now the bartender. What is going on here?

Before I can think any more about it, the lights and music shut off simultaneously. Groans and complaints rise from the crowd, but the main lights soon come back on. The music, however, does not. I know this is my sign.

I stand on top of the bar. "Attention, assholes!" I yell. All heads turn to me, and I take out my gun. Some people gasp. Others scream. I smile. "I'm sorry to inform you that you are all going to die!"

I turn to the bartender, about to put him at gunpoint for the money, but that's when I hear it: the chatter of a police radio coming from behind the bar. "The suspect is within range," it says. "In position to apprehend." That's when I notice the radio on the bartender's hip. His eyes widen when I take notice of it. I realize what's happening. The bartender is a cop, and I bet the bouncer is too, and likely several other people here. That's why they let us in without question. They wanted us in here, a confined space, easy to apprehend. This whole thing is a setup. I see him reaching for his weapon, and in an instant, I point the gun at his skull and shoot him dead. I hear a few members of the crowd gasp, and nobody moves.

I make eye contact with Alejandro across the room, and he widens his eyes in question.

"It's a trap!" I yell and jump down from the bar, hoping to shoot my way through the crowd. For all I know or care, everyone in here is trying to kill me. Everyone here is an enemy. Gunfire goes off, and it feels like it's coming from every direction. That's when the crowd goes completely ballistic, with people running in every direction, screaming, crying. I decide to take advantage of the chaos and make my way through the crowd. I holster my gun and throw my leather jacket off in an attempt to blend in. There's no point in trying to complete the job now. We just have to do our best not to get caught. Anger saps my focus, and all I can think about is the failed mission. The government has ruined yet another of my attempts to avenge Natalie. I try to make my way to the back door, where we planned to meet the gang. There are cries of "Oh my god!" and "What's going on?" before one man stands on top of the bar with a gun, flashing a badge. Shit.

"Nashville City Police Department! Please, everyone calm down!" he hollers. His voice is a deep boom over the chaos ensuing down below. The hysteria stops momentarily, the police officer giving the crowd an illusion of safety. "Any and all individuals involved in the break-in of Fort Knox, stand down!"

The crowd waits for someone to say something or step up, but of course, no one does. However, this gives me an idea. Maybe there is a way for me to get some recognition from this job. Not only will I have witnesses now, but I'll get a full witness report from several cops as well. I'm only about twenty yards away from the cop. I take my gun out of its holster and shoot the cop in the head. He falls down from the bar, and the chaos resumes.

I see a black speaker and run toward it. Juan and Eduardo were shutting off the music, so they should be near the speakers.

I whip my head around and spot a bright red polo, just like the one Juan was wearing. It might be a long shot, but I run toward it and see Juan and Eduardo hidden behind the sound booth. Juan is crouched down, and when I see Eduardo, my breath catches in my throat. He has a bullet wound to his right calf. He is sitting down with his leg extended. Juan is saying something to him, then he catches my gaze. He motions for me to come over to them. I crouch down next to Juan and see the dead cop on the other side of the sound box. Eduardo groans.

"What the fuck happened?!" I scream at Juan. With all the noise, I'm not even sure if he hears me, but he seems to have gotten the message that I'm not happy.

Juan speaks loudly and I can just make out what he's saying over all the commotion. "Eduardo and I were trying to shut off the music, and as soon as we did, a cop came and shot him." He glances over to the dead body next to him. "I killed the cop."

I contemplate leaving him, but knowing Eduardo, he would help the police in order to stay alive. Even if he were to bleed out from his wounds before the police were able to capture him, he would still likely have evidence on his person tying him back to the gang.

"We need to get Eduardo out of here right now," I say and turn to Eduardo. "This isn't going to feel good, but you are going to run out of here with Juan and me." Eduardo just groans in response, and I assume that means he doesn't oppose the idea, so Juan puts Eduardo's arm over his shoulders, and I begin to guide them out.

We make it to the back door, and I see that Alejandro, as well as two other members of the gang, are making their way to the door as well, firing the occasional shot at an enemy I can't see. When Alejandro catches my gaze, he runs toward us.

"Thank god!" Alejandro exclaims when he sees us, then looks at Eduardo. His relieved expression turns to horror. "What happened? Is he going to be OK?"

"Not if we don't get him out of here," I say, annoyed at how this all went south. I move out of the way so that another member of the gang can help support Eduardo in my place. "Let's go!" Alejandro opens the door, and we run out. But of course, with our luck, we don't make it more than a few steps before we see two cops standing there with their guns pointed at us.

One of them has pale skin and light brown hair up in a bun; the other has dark skin, and her black hair is braided and tied up into a ponytail. I notice that neither of them has her gun pointed at Juan, or Alejandro, or anyone else in the gang. They both point their weapons directly at me. My gun is holstered, and they could shoot me three times over before I could grab it. The only thing I can do is put my hands up.

"Kendall Cooper," says the cop with the light brown hair. "I am Detective Toole, and you're under arrest."

CHAPTER TWENTY-SIX

DANIELLE

It doesn't feel real. The girl that I have been tracking, studying, obsessing over, is right here in front of me. She looks different than any other time I've seen her. She's wearing makeup, and her hair and outfit make her look older. But still, I recognize her. Her hands are above her head, yet she doesn't look defeated. Her gaze is unwavering and fixed on me. The intensity of her stare surprises me, but I maintain my composure. Containing my emotions is one of the things I've learned to do well in my years as a detective.

There are five people beside her. One has taken a bullet to the leg and is being supported by another two, none of whom seem to be much of a threat. The last two, however, are armed and don't seem too eager to surrender. One of the men has an automatic rifle and begins to lift it. Nicki has quicker reflexes than him and aims her gun at him while mine remains on Cooper.

"Hey!" she yells authoritatively. "Put it down." The man has a steady hold on the gun but seems to recognize that Nicki would be able to shoot him quicker than he could aim it at her and fire. He slowly sets the gun down and puts his hands up. I suppose we've found ourselves in something of a stalemate. Nicki and I can't aim at the other criminals, because the ones we have now would get away. However, the criminals can't aim their weapons toward us because even if they succeeded in killing one of us, the other would kill them instantly. The others would likely get away, but whoever made the first move would basically be sacrificing themselves. We all stand there for a long time, trying to figure out what to do.

Just as I take one hand off my gun to reach for my radio and call for backup, one of the men throws his gun at Nicki. My immediate thought is how stupid he is for throwing away his weapon like that. However, I see that this is a calculated move. It is enough to stun her and shock us both, giving him an opening to tackle me to the ground. My gun goes flying, and I hear it land a few yards behind me.

"Alejandro!" one of the men yells, and I hear a taser fire. Nicki must have stunned one of the criminals, and the man on top of me, whom I assume is Alejandro, throws a punch at me. Panic sets in, and without my gun, I can't defend myself. He hits me, and pain shoots through my face. I try to get up, shimmying out from under him a bit, but the man, Alejandro, pushes me back down onto my stomach, twisting my arm so that I stay down.

"Stop," He says. "I don't want to hurt you. Let my men go, and I won't." Fear courses through my veins. I consider the idea for a moment. Alejandro is a lot bigger than me, and clearly a better fighter. I should let the lot of them go if I want to live. But then I see Kendall Cooper standing just feet away from me. I see her watching us. I remember everything I learned about her. I remember who she was and who she is now. An idea begins to form in my head. A stupid, independent, dangerous idea. I push the idea away.

My hands eventually find their way into making fists, and I can see Nicki out of the corner of my eye. Her gun is pointed at the criminals. They are still threats, and even if they weren't, I doubt she would take a shot at Alejandro for fear of shooting me in the scuffle. It's up to me to apprehend him. The idea takes over my brain again. My desire to do good is going to get me killed. I know that I can't let morals get in the way of my job, but this idea seems so plausible. The image of Cooper behind bars comes into my mind again. It still seems entirely wrong. The power is in my hands. This is it. This is my opportunity to give Kendall Cooper a chance no one else will ever give her.

I feel Alejandro's force on my arm lessening. He thinks I will let him go. I take the opportunity to escape his grip and punch him in the face, with all my strength. To my surprise, he falls to the ground. I hardly have time to react, I need to be quick about this. I reach into my belt and pull out a small wire. I quickly stand up and grab his foot, twisting it so he can't get up. I interlace the wire into the shoelaces of Alejandro's black tennis shoes. He squirms and kicks, and finally a kick from his other foot lands on my chest. I tumble backward, being sure to catch Nicki as I fall to the ground. She stumbles and falls under me. That's when a navy blue van I didn't notice before rumbles to life. I act as if I'm trying to get up while staying on top of Nicki.

I let the group of people, including Kendall Cooper, get away.

They get in the van, and just as they speed away, I slowly get to my feet and make half an effort to run after it. Nicki follows. The van quickly speeds out of view, and we both stop.

"Damn it!" Nicki yells. She turns to me. "Are you OK? You didn't get the license plate, did you?"

"No," I say. "All I saw was the letter V." This was one of the few things I knew were inevitably to come that wasn't a lie. I try to hide the uneasiness that is beginning to grow inside me. What have I just done? I betrayed everything I stand for. I betrayed the oath I took when I began my job. *What have I done?*

Thankfully, Nicki distracts me. "You're bleeding," she says, gesturing to my nose. I put my hand to my nose and feel the warm blood. The adrenaline in my system is wearing off, and I'm beginning to feel the impact of the fist to my face. I guess my reaction to Alejandro's blows weren't all theater. "Come on, let's get you fixed up."

~

Several ambulances arrive minutes after the criminals sped away, along with an extensive amount of law enforcement officers. If I were really trying to catch the group of criminals, I would have been angry that they hadn't been here in the first place. However, underestimating them has worked to my advantage.

The paramedic shines a light in my eye. She clicks the flashlight off and begins to poke and prod at my nose before finally cleaning the blood off.

"So?" I ask, praying that she clears me to work.

"You don't have a concussion," she says. "Or a broken nose. Just a good old whack to the face. You're fine."

"Thank you," I say, hopping down from the back of the ambulance and walking over to Nicki, who is waiting impatiently for me.

"You OK?" she asks. "He got you pretty good."

"I'm fine," I say. "Nothing serious."

"Good," she says. "I haven't seen Agent Danvers anywhere, which is unusual for her. What's our next move? Question the witnesses? Collect evidence?"

"We need to go back to the station," I say. "Like, right now."

"What?" Nicki asks. Her tone matches the confusion on her face. "Why? Aren't we supposed to help here?"

I hesitate. I have to tell Nicki about this. She's my partner, and even more than that, she's my friend. I'm just not sure how she'll react. When I betrayed the oath, I pulled her down with me, without even considering how she felt about it. I'm beginning to think this was all a bad idea.

"I can't explain right now," I say quickly. "You just need to trust me. I promise I will explain everything when we get back to the station." Nicki's expression is something in between concerned and confused, but she nods, and we get in the car.

~

When we get to my desk, the station is completely empty, which I am grateful for. "OK, so what are you being so secretive about?" Nicki says.

I bite my bottom lip. "I let them go." Nicki's mouth falls open, and she seems to be debating whether to say something or if she heard me right at all.

"What?" she says, her voice reflecting the utter disbelief that is registering on her face.

"The criminals, with Cooper and..." I trail off. Was Kendall Cooper worth all of this? "I let them go. I could have arrested that man, Alejandro, but I didn't. I let them go." I find myself sounding a little more confident this time.

"Dani... I—" Nicki stutters. "What? Why would you do that?"

I can sense her getting angry at me, and I quickly try to recover. "Let me explain."

"Explain what? You know what these people are capable of!" she says, her voice more scared than angry, which does not put me at ease. "*I* know what these people are capable of. Why would you let them go? This could have been our one chance!" Now she was drifting more into an angry tone. I put my hands up defensively.

"That's not what I did at all. I didn't arrest him but," I say, trying to keep my voice calm. I pull a case from my belt and open it to reveal that its contents are gone. "I bugged Alejandro's shoe."

CHAPTER TWENTY-SEVEN

KENDALL

I press down harder on the bullet wound in Eduardo's leg. He lets out a yelp and a whole lot of complaining, but I snap at him to shut up. Every single cell in my body is fuming with rage. If I have to take that rage out on Eduardo's leg wound, so be it. It will stop the bleeding, anyway.

"Kendall..." Alejandro begins cautiously.

"I need to press down hard to stop the bleeding," I snap at him. "Don't you think I've ever been shot before?" Alejandro nods and goes back to cleaning his gun. I think he likes to distract himself from things like this. Honestly, I feel worse for him than I do for Eduardo. Seeing a sibling in pain is probably the worst thing a person can experience. I would know. God, I would fucking know. Another reminder that I have failed yet again to avenge my sister.

We hit a bump in the road, and Eduardo whimpers again. It takes everything in me not to punch him, and I press down even harder on the wound. After about five minutes, the van slows to a stop, and I hear all the gang members in the front get out. I think there are four, plus Juan, and after the doors shut, I hear their footsteps getting fainter and fainter. Once I can't hear them anymore, Alejandro glances at Eduardo and me nervously.

"We'll be fine back here," I say, my tone anything but reassuring. Even so, Alejandro knows me, and no matter how angry I am, I wouldn't let an ally as valuable to me as Eduardo die.

~

After about half an hour, the van comes to a screeching halt. I wait for the door to open and hear the signature *tap! Tap! Tap!* This is the safe signal. With that, I stand up and, with great effort, help Eduardo to his feet. I try not to think about Natalie's last night when I sling his arm over my shoulder. Although the movement is so similar, the context so familiar. I've never been particularly fond of Eduardo, but he has proven himself useful time and time again. As annoyed with him as I get, I realize that I don't want him to die.

Alejandro opens the doors of the van and gets in. We didn't even bother to cover our tracks this time, since we needed to get Eduardo to safety as soon as possible. We can just clean the guns and dispose of them tomorrow.

Alejandro hops into the van and slings Eduardo's other arm over his shoulders, and together we help him out of the van. We are approaching the front steps of the house when Cecelia runs out, her expression filled with shock and horror.

"Dios mío!" she exclaims, putting her hand on her chest. She's too nice. If I was in her shoes, after all the horrible things Eduardo has said and threatened to do to her, I'd laugh.

"Cecelia," Alejandro says. "He needs first aid." He needs a little more than first aid, but I don't say so. I think Cecelia knows this too, but to put Alejandro at ease, she nods and runs into the house.

Getting Eduardo up the steps to the front porch is no easy feat, and it takes us almost five minutes to reach the front door. By then I have noticed two things. One, Eduardo is much heavier than he looks. Two, the bleeding has slowed, so he's going to be fine.

As we walk in the front door, Milo seems to realize that some-thing is wrong and keeps his distance. He's such a smart dog. We lay Eduardo down on the couch, and Cecelia comes out of the bathroom with the first aid kit. The bullet went completely through Eduardo's leg, and the blood is already beginning to clot. The only thing we will have to do is sanitize it, then sew it up and bandage it.

Cecelia opens the first aid kit, and I notice something in her other hand: a sewing kit. She has sewn up my clothes a couple of times after they've been torn up on jobs, and I know that she's the only one with a steady enough hand to sew up the wound. Her eyes are wide with fear, and she looks at me. I give her a nod of encouragement, and she hesitantly nods back.

I quickly clean the wound with rubbing alcohol, causing Eduardo to cry out. I tell him to shut up and hold down his arms, instructing Alejandro to hold down his legs. I don't tell him what we are going to do; all I tell him is that it's going to hurt. I don't think Eduardo has ever expressed any sort of fear of needles, but anyone would be terrified if they knew they were going to get sewn up like a stuffed animal.

I'm practically sitting on Eduardo's limbs when Cecelia gets back from the kitchen after sanitizing the needle and threads it. She takes a deep breath before she pierces his skin. The moment it touches him, Eduardo lets out an ear-splitting scream that nearly deafens me. Everyone for miles must have heard that.

Eduardo squirms and tries to get free of Alejandro and me, but he's too weak. Cecelia pulls the thread through, and I'm hoping that when she makes contact for the second time, Eduardo's reaction will be less dramatic.

It isn't.

The same scream follows the second time, and I can feel my right ear ringing. His scream is the most shrill little girl sound I have ever heard. I can't take it anymore. If he keeps this up, we will never be able to treat him, and frankly, it is annoying as shit.

"Stop!" I yell, and Cecelia obeys. I take my hands off of his arms, and Eduardo relaxes. He gasps for air.

"Thank you..." He takes another breath. "Kendall." I walk over to the kitchen.

"What happened?" Cecelia asks. "Did I do something wrong?"

"No," I say, with my back turned to her. I grab a frying pan from the pile of dirty dishes in the sink. "You're doing great." I walk back over to where Eduardo is lying on the couch.

Eduardo doesn't see me, but Alejandro does. His eyes go wide. "Kendall, what are you—" But he doesn't have time to finish before I knock Eduardo out cold with the frying pan.

~

Half an hour later, the stitching is done, the wound is bandaged, Eduardo is unconscious but alive, and everyone else is exhausted. Taking care of an injured Eduardo is like taking care of a child. Part of me wishes that we left him at the club to spare my ears.

I sit on the floor in front of the TV, petting Milo. "Are you OK?" I hear Cecelia ask Alejandro behind me.

"Yes," he says. "I'm OK, I just...seeing him in pain is hard." Sometimes I wonder how they can possibly just talk to each other like that. Just share their emotions out loud and not even worry about how the information could be used against them. I wonder if I'll have that someday. Once the thought enters my head, another thought comes to replace it. Definitely not. If I'm going to avenge Natalie, I can't let anyone get in the way. No matter how much I trust them or care about them.

"Why don't we watch the news?" Cecelia suggests. "Maybe you will be on it." I can almost see her warm smile.

"Sure," Alejandro says, using the tone he only ever uses with Cecelia. "Why not." The TV clicks on, and I look up to see the news reporter sitting at her fancy blue desk.

"Breaking news," she says in her annoying news voice. "The minor suspected of involvement in the robbery at Fort Knox, Kendall Cooper, has been spotted again in a popular nightclub in downtown Nashville." My heart skips a beat, and I turn my head to look at Alejandro. He points the remote at the TV and turns the volume up. Could this really have worked? "The suspect is described as being a young Caucasian female with dirty blonde hair, and hazel eyes approximately 5'4". If you have any information on the suspect, please contact your local law enforcement." The news goes on to an interview with a cop at the scene, but I barely hear it. This is what I wanted this whole time. Ma'am and Sir are sure to see this. I'm sure Fort Knox raised their suspicions, and this without a doubt tells them it was me. But the rush of victory never comes. Instead, this news segment is bringing back a memory. A memory of something important.

I'm back there. I'm back at one of the first houses I ever lived at. I'm five. I walk up to Natalie, who's ten. We're packing our room up into boxes.

"Nat," I say. "Why are we leaving?"

"One of our siblings got arrested," she says. "David. You wouldn't remember him. You were young when he left."

"David," I repeat. "Why does that mean we have to move?"

"Well, he left the organization a long time ago," she says. "But he still has information about us, and it's dangerous to stay here. We're going to stay at a private booth at a basketball stadium tonight. There's a game. After that, we're going to find a new place to live."

The world comes back to me, and I hear Alejandro calling my name. "Hey, kid," he says. "You OK?"

Whenever a member of the Clan was caught, or information about them was released to the public, we would move, but there was never enough time to find a new home. We would always stay in the Southeast, so we would go somewhere readily accessible to us. We would always stay in the same private booth in a basketball stadium for a night or two until we got everything in order. I'm not technically a part of the Mors Clan anymore, so it never even occurred to me that my family would go there after my information was revealed, but this memory is telling me otherwise. My goal of recognition pales in comparison to the knowledge of the Clan's location.

"I need to use the computer," I say, and before either Alejandro or Cecelia can say anything, I run to the junk room. I sit down and head to the stadium's site to look up a list of the people who purchased tickets for the game tomorrow night. Ma'am and Sir had contacts in the industry, so they were always able to get tickets. The site doesn't let me in, because I need some type of authorization to see the people who are going, and I remember that Eduardo has a flash drive that contains some hacking software. I rummage through the drawers until I find the bright red flash drive I'm looking for.

I plug it into the computer, and it begins to tear down the firewalls. It takes less than a minute before I'm in. I scroll through the ticket list—there must be hundreds of people on it—until I find two names that catch my eye.

John and Cynthia Moore.

Those were two of Ma'am and Sir's aliases. Their most common ones, in fact. I gasp lightly and chuckle. My heart flutters with hope, and for the first time ever, I feel the urge to cry happy tears. I put my hand on the screen, as if trying to make sure the names don't go anywhere. I know where my parents are. And if I know where they are, I can kill them. This is it. I can avenge Natalie. I can finally give her some justice. I smile. Ma'am always did say I was the most skilled of her children.

My smile turns to a smirk as I begin to speak.

"I'm going to make you proud, Ma'am."

~

"Are you insane?" Alejandro yells, then massages his temples. "You are insane. You are actually insane. Do you not remember what happened tonight at the club? It was a disaster! The feds are onto us. We need to leave!"

"No!" I scream, and the cabin is completely silent. I try to speak more calmly this time. "You don't understand. This job is essential to solidify our image. We need to show them we're not afraid. Then I promise we will leave the country, and we will never have to go on a job again." This is mostly a lie, but I can't tell him the truth. I can't tell him about my family, and the Clan, and Natalie. He would never understand.

"We *are* never going on a job again," he says, his voice quieter but just as intense. "Not in this country. We have to get out."

"We will!" I yell. "After this job!"

"Absolutely not!" Alejandro argues back, matching my tone. "Eduardo could have died tonight!"

"He didn't!" I holler. "He's fine!"

"But he could have!" Alejandro says. "Our last job was a setup; we cannot risk another one. We have to think logically."

"I am!" I snap. "I always think logically! I got you into goddamn Fort Knox! I made you rich; hell, I even got you jobs after that without you or anyone you care about getting caught!"

"Really?" he says. "Because it came pretty damn close this time! What exactly is your plan, genius?"

I'm a little shocked that Alejandro is speaking with so much venom, especially toward me. I have never seen him so angry.

"We will go to the St. Williams Basketball Stadium in time for the 7:00 p.m. game," I say. "We will enter through the side entrance, where there is no alarm wired. I'll pick the lock, and we will be under the bleachers. We will place remotely activated bombs under the bleachers and run out before we blow the whole place up. It's simple!"

Alejandro smirks. "You forgot about the part where we get caught. Or worse, we die."

"That isn't going to happen," I say. "Because I am making the plan! You should know that my plans always work."

"*You* are on the news!" he yells. "Every person in the country is out looking for you, and who's to say that if they predicted where we'd be last time, they can't predict it this time?"

"We wanted recognition! And nonetheless, we're still alive!" I yell. "You can't act like you never knew this was dangerous. You always knew what we were up against!"

That silences him for a few moments. "Eduardo almost died tonight," he says, his voice surprisingly quiet. "What if next time we go on a job, he actually does, or I do, or you do? Don't you understand? I'm trying to do what's best for all of us. For this *family*." There is silence between us as I replay the word he just uttered. Family. *Family*. Family has brought me nothing but pain my entire life. All a family does is tear you down and hurt you in ways no one else can. Family makes you weak and vulnerable. I will never have a family again.

"Well," I say. "I am going to do this with or without your help." I begin to walk out of the kitchen and to my room before I stop and look back over my shoulder at Alejandro. "And you're not my family." Alejandro looks at me like I just slapped him. Then his expression hardens.

"Well, if you're not family, then maybe you should leave," he says, his voice stone cold. "Your obsession with these jobs has put all of us in danger. You're out of the gang." Now it's my turn to feel like someone just struck me. I turn to look at him. I feel as if someone has just beaten me to a pulp and I'm just lying there, dazed.

"What?" I say, so quietly it's almost a whisper.

"Alejandro—" Cecelia says, coming to his side. From her tone, she's going to try to talk him out of this.

"My decision is final," he says, cutting her off. Alejandro begins to walk toward his bedroom but then stops a few feet from me.

He doesn't look at me, but I look at his expression. For a moment, it looks like he's about to tell me to stay, that I can stay in this house, the only place in the world where I actually care about the people in it. But the moment passes.

"I'm going to bed. By the time I wake up tomorrow, I want you gone." He storms past me and into his bedroom. I'm left in shock, unable to even think about what my next move will be. I just stand there.

CHAPTER TWENTY-EIGHT

DANIELLE

I replay the audio, not truly believing what was recorded. I replay it again. And again. And again.

"We will go to the St. Williams Basketball Stadium," Kendall Cooper's voice says on the recording. "We will enter through the side entrance where there is no alarm wired. I'll pick the lock, and we will be under the bleachers. We will place remotely activated bombs under the bleachers and run out before we blow the whole place up. It's simple!"

I hear Nicki behind me. "Would you *please* stop that?" she says, clearly annoyed with me replaying the audio.

"Sorry," I say sheepishly. "I just—I mean, I can't believe it. We got her. This is what we've been looking for. We have her now."

"We need to inform Agent Danvers," Nicki says. "She can get a squad there in time. We need to make up for *your* mistake." Nicki begins to walk to her desk, but I stand up and grab her arm. She seems surprised by the gesture and turns to me.

"What if we didn't?" I suggest. The same stupid idea that has taken root in my head begins to branch off into a different one. An even more dangerous one, if that's possible.

"What?!" Nicki exclaims, then her expression hardens. "If you can't arrest her, then I will."

"She's alone now," I say. "There won't be anyone to talk her out of it. We can help her."

"Just like *you* wanted to," Nicki corrects. Ouch. "There's no way we can actually just let her go. This kid needs to be locked up. Anything besides that is going to end with a lot of blood on our hands."

"She doesn't deserve to be arrested," I say, interrupting her. "I believe that. Her whole life, she was forced into crime. She didn't have a choice—no one in her family did. If she didn't kill, she would die. And clearly she didn't *like* it. Otherwise she wouldn't have run away. But then her sister died, and now she's falling back into crime because of it." Nicki is completely silent. "She doesn't need to be arrested. She needs help. And we might be the only people in the world that can give her that."

"And how would you propose we do that?" She asks. "How would we possibly be able to help a criminal?"

"We go to the stadium tomorrow night, and we talk to her," I say.

"Talking to her?" Nicki says, her tone almost pitying. "Do you think that will undo the *years* of trauma that turned her into a killer? Dani, if we try to talk to her, she's going to kill us."

"I know how she feels," I blurt out. As soon as I say it, I wish I hadn't. "A very important person in her life was taken from her, and she feels completely alone in the world. If I show her that she's not, maybe we can get her into witness protection, and she could give us information on her parents' crime organization. We could help *more* people this way. Think about it." Nicki is silent for a minute, and I can tell she's considering it. "She got kicked out of her gang; she feels lost and abandoned. She's more likely to trust us now than ever before. This might be our only chance."

She crosses her arms over her chest, and when she finally speaks, her tone is soft.

"I can tell that I won't be able to talk you out of this," she says. "And as much as I don't like it, you're my partner and my best friend. I'm not going to let you rush into danger alone."

I give Nicki a half-hearted smile and try not to show how unsure I am about this.

"Thank you," I say.

CHAPTER TWENTY-NINE

KENDALL

I walk into my room, knowing that it's the last time it will ever be *my* room. Milo is lying on my bed, and when he sees me, he thumps his tail. My heart sinks. I know he can't come with me. There's no way I can take care of him, and he wouldn't be safe. I sigh and sit down next to him. He's so innocent. So sweet and loving. He deserves someone better than me. I stroke his little head.

"I know you don't understand this," I say softly, "but I'm going to have to leave now. I promise Cecelia will take good care of you." I pause. "Better care than I ever did." I can feel tears welling in the corners of my eyes, but I blink them away. Crying never did anyone any good. I swallow my grief over losing Milo and stand up. I grab my duffel bag off the floor and take all the clothes I have out of it. I won't need them anymore. I'll need somewhere to put the parts for the bomb though. I zip it up and sling it over my shoulder.

I go to the doorway to exit the room and look back one last time. I know that if I keep dwelling on the loss of it, I'll never leave. So I turn away and walk into the kitchen, where Cecelia is sitting at the table. Her head is in her hands, and I'm not sure if I should say something or not.

Luckily, she makes the decision for me when she sees me enter.

"Come here, honey," she says, her voice as kind as ever. I walk over to the table but don't sit down. I remind myself that I don't live here anymore.

"Thank you," I say quietly. "For everything." Cecelia shakes her head.

"No," she says with tears in her eyes. "Having you here was a gift." I smile. I'll miss her. She stands up and lowers her voice. "I'll take you where you need to go."

This offer surprises me. Cecelia sides with Alejandro on most matters. I doubt he would approve of her helping me.

"Thank you," is all I can say. She leads me outside and to the van, which she starts up. I sit in the passenger seat.

"Where do you want to go?" she asks. I realize I don't really know. I doubt she wants Alejandro to know that she helped me, and the game isn't until tomorrow night, so I think of the one other person in the world that might help me.

"A member of the gang," I say. "His name is Juan. Do you know where he lives?"

"I do," she says and begins to drive. "I doubt he's up right now, but I'll take you."

The drive is mostly silent. Neither of us knows what to say. What do you say? I was just kicked out of her house, and she's going to flee the country. I know I'm never going to see her again, and we're not even ending on good terms. What am I supposed to say to that? I want to ask her if she'll take care of Milo for me, but I don't want to ask any more of her than I already have. She's helping me against Alejandro's wishes. That's more than I would have asked for already.

"I don't know if you knew this," Cecelia says, "but I can't have kids."

"Oh," I say softly.

"Having you in our house..." She pauses. "It has been a bless-ing." She looks at me, and for the first time, I recognize how brave she is. "You have been a better daughter than I could ever wish for."

I smile at her, and again I feel the tears about to come, but I remember my place.

I say, "I'm sorry it all had to end like this, but I'm glad I got to know you."

"Me too," she says and turns a corner, pulling up in front of a small brown one-story house. She stops the car and looks at me again with her sad, brave eyes. "I guess this is goodbye then." I nod.

"I guess it is," I say, and I can feel myself sink. I had never realized what an important person Cecelia has become in my life until right now. "I wish I could...put into words how grateful I am for everything you've done for me."

"You don't have to, honey," she says. "And I know you don't like hugs, but I don't care." She pulls me in for a hug, and I hug her back. I find myself not wanting to let go, but I know I have to. I have to remind myself of what is truly important. This job. I grab my duffel and get out of the van. I close the door. I will myself not to feel anything as I watch through the window of the van as the last piece of my old life drives away.

I sigh. This past year has been nice, but now that I think about it, living with Alejandro, Eduardo, and Cecelia would never have worked with my plan. They were nice, but their goals were too small, and even before Eduardo got shot, they were too quick to run from a fight. I've let myself become distracted by them, by their kindness and their desire to help me. I stare at the one hundred dollars in my hand. We were going to work out my cut from Fort Knox, but with the whirlwind that came afterward, we never got around to it. Stupid. I feel guilty for stealing from Cecelia, but I know that if she knew what it would be used for, she wouldn't have given it to me. It occurred to me on the ride over that I don't know how to build a bomb that will remotely detonate. If I am going to kill my parents, I am going to have to die too. The price of my life is one I'm willing to pay to avenge Natalie. I walk up to the front door and knock until Juan finally opens it.

"Kendall," Juan says, sounding surprised. In the dark, I can't make out his expression. "What are you doing here?"

"You said you would help me, right?" I say. Juan seems surprised by the mention of our conversation at the dugout that day, but eventually, I see his silhouette nod. "Then let's go."

"What happened?" Juan asks.

"Alejandro kicked me out of the gang," I say, as if I couldn't care less. "I need you to drive me somewhere." I can only imagine Juan's shocked expression, and he doesn't say anything for a long time. I wonder if he even meant it when he said he would help me.

"Where do you want me to take you?"

~

I rummage through the back room of Bradley's shop. Honestly, I'm not even surprised that it's still open at this hour. It must be about three in the morning right now. I feel the money in my pocket, and guilt makes my chest clench. After all the good things Cecelia did for me, in return I stole from her. Was this all worth it? Am I making the right choice in my mission to avenge Natalie?

"I love you, more than anything." Natalie's voice rings in my ears, as if she is standing right next to me. "And that's why you have to go." The guilt in my chest expands, threatening to swallow me whole. What would Natalie think if she saw what I've become? What would she say when she realized the lengths to which I've gone to avenge her?

I drown out the thoughts in my head with a single sentence. She would have done the same for me. Just like Natalie was the most important person in my life, I was the most important person in hers. She would have done anything for me. I know it. Still, the feeling that I'm doing the wrong thing doesn't leave me.

"You building a bomb?" Bradley asks. His voice makes me jump, and I realize I must have been staring at the same wall of bolts for ages.

"What happened to your don't ask, don't tell policy?" I ask, glaring at him.

"Well, I know how to build a bomb," he says. "I'm not an idiot. Plus, you've been standing there doing absolutely nothing for minutes now."

"Sorry," is all I can say as I grab the type of bolts I need. That's the last thing I need to make the bomb. I take everything and set it on the counter.

"That's $89.56," he says, then gives me a knowing look. "Or a little more if you want me to keep quiet about this." I take the money out of my pocket, knowing I don't have the money he wants for the information to stay with him.

You're going to die, I remind myself. *You don't need to cover your tracks.*

"No, thanks," I say. "Just the parts." Bradley looks confused for a moment, but he's smart. I know that he knows if I'm OK with leaving a trail, I'm either going to die, or I'm planning on getting caught. Either way, it means I won't be back. He just nods and takes the money from my hand. I put the parts in my duffel and walk out the door. No turning back now.

I hop into the small two-seater car, where Juan is waiting for me. "Did you get what you need?" he asks.

"Yes," I say.

"Where do we need to go?"

"Not *we,*" I say. "Just me. St. Williams Stadium." He nods and begins to drive. That's when the full impact of the day hits me. Between the argument with Alejandro, the job, and the fact that I haven't slept in over 20 hours, I realize that I am exhausted. My eyelids begin to droop. I can trust Juan enough to sleep, right? If his goal was to betray me in any way, why help me at all?

"How long is the drive?"

"About an hour," he says. "Why?" An hour of sleep sounds amazing right now.

"Would it be OK if I slept for a little bit?" I ask.

"Sure," he says. Once I close my eyes, it takes no time at all for me to drift off.

~

Befitting the circumstances, when I sleep tonight, I dream of the night Natalie was killed. Turn it to the right. 37. Turn it to the left. Pass it once. 13. Turn it to the right one more time. 42. Natalie opens the safe and gives me the half-completed plans for Fort Knox. Then I relive my own personal hell. How our plan went so horribly wrong.

We open the door. The alarm system goes off. The footsteps upstairs. Us running. My stomach to the forest floor as I calculate my chance of survival. The twig snapping.

The twig.

When it snaps, I feel a crunch under my foot. Gunfire unloads into the woods, and I wake up with a gasp. Cold sweat covers me, and my whole body trembles. I grip the side of the passenger seat so hard that the fabric tears. A choking sob threatens to come spilling out of my throat. It was me. I stepped on that twig. I killed Natalie. There aren't words to describe what I'm feeling right now. I feel like I'm frozen. My emotions stun me completely, and I couldn't move if I tried. I killed Natalie. It was my fault. I may as well have murdered my own sister. I don't know how long I sit there, frozen in time, horrorstruck, reliving my dream. Then, as if a switch has been flipped, my panic recedes, and an eerie calm comes over me.

Now I know I made the right choice.

CHAPTER THIRTY

DANIELLE

We drive around the stadium five times in the squad car, until we identify exactly which door Kendall Cooper is going to go in. We found the blueprints of the stadium last night, and there are only a few doors that are not wired to an alarm: the front door and three side doors. However, one of the side doors is considerably more accessible than the others. It's my best guess that the one to the far right of the main entrance, where people are pouring into the stadium, is where Kendall Cooper will enter, or has already entered. I check my watch.

"Game starts in ten minutes," I say, turning to Nicki. "She's probably already inside." Nicki's brow furrows with worry, and I begin to go through all the possible scenarios in my mind.

Nicki puts a hand on my shoulder. "Just...buzz me and I'll come rushing in," she says. I nod. We decided that one of us would go in, and if something went wrong, the other would call for backup before coming to help. I set my radio to a private channel between Nicki and me. If something goes wrong and I need her to come in after me, I just press the button on the side of the radio twice. However, I doubt that Kendall Cooper will be friendly when she sees me, so buzzing Nicki has to be my last resort. Maybe this wasn't such a good plan after all.

This could go one of three ways. One, I convince Cooper to help us end the Mors Clan and come with me. She would assume a fake identity, dye her hair, make her appearance completely different, and hopefully her information would lead to the capture of her parents and the end of the Cooper family's role in their crime organization. Two, Kendall Cooper kills me and ends up going through with her plan to blow up the basketball stadium, killing potentially hundreds of people. Three, I get to the point that I know I can't stop Kendall Cooper, and I have to buzz Nicki. I can only hope that the first scenario is the one that plays out.

But I can't think about all the what-ifs right now. I need to stop thinking like a detective and start thinking like a cop. I have to think about the here and the now, and most importantly, I have to stay true to my objective. I have to convince Kendall Cooper to help us.

I know that if I wait until I'm ready, I'll never get out of the car, so I just get out anyway. "Good luck," Nicki says quietly as I leave. "Be careful."

"I always am," I say teasingly. The thing that bothers me is that it used to be true. How have I let this girl, this one case, change me so much? I close the door before I can think about it any more. I begin to walk around the stadium to the door where Kendall Cooper is—with her bomb.

~

I stand in front of the door. The door to the stadium. Behind the door is potentially one of the most dangerous people in the country. Once I open this door, I will have officially betrayed my oath, and I will never be able to go back. The only comfort to me is that I am still apprehending a criminal. My end goal is to bring down a crime organization, although if I'm found out, I doubt it will be seen that way.

I grab the cold door handle and pull it down. It doesn't move. She must have locked it again. I grab a bobby pin from my hair and stick it in the lock. I wiggle it around a few times, and it unlocks. It's not a very strong lock, but then again, I doubt the people who designed it considered it would be used for this. I pull out my gun and aim it forward.

I open the door.

When I walk in, Kendall Cooper is standing there, and my heart skips a beat when I find myself staring down the barrel of her handgun. I point my own gun at her. I can see her eyes fluttering to me, out the door, then back to me. Then a glint of recognition registers, and I know she remembers me from the club.

"I don't want to hurt you," I say.

"Really? That's funny, 'cause I happen to be staring at the business end of your gun," Kendall retorts. She's right. There's no way she'll listen to me if she views me as an active threat. Her eyes flicker back to the door, and I realize what she's thinking. People are still entering the stadium for the game. If she shoots me, people will hear it and come running. She'll have to set off her bomb too soon, and there won't be as many people in the stands as there would be once the game starts. Which I'm sure is when she plans to set off the bomb. She won't kill me, because if she does, it will ruin her entire plan. There's a chance she'll hold off on killing me long enough for me to get through to her. I put my gun back in its holster.

"Let me explain," I say.

There's a long pause as she considers, and finally, Cooper tightens her grip on her gun. "You have thirty seconds before I kill you."

I take the opportunity gratefully.

"My name is Danielle, and I know about what happened to you," I say, my words practically tripping over themselves. "I know about your parents. I know you hated being involved in the Mors Clan. I know you ran away. I know about Natalie. And everyone in the world wants you arrested. Everyone in the world wants to see you pay for your crimes, but I can help you." An emotion I can't make out floods Kendall's face. My stomach squeezes with anticipation for what's to come. Either a cry of compliance, or a bullet through my chest.

"How do I know you're not just stalling until your backup comes to arrest me?" Kendall Cooper yells. Her tone is fierce, but I can sense a hint of uncertainty underlying it.

"I can hardly imagine what you've been through in your childhood," I say. "But with your sister..." I hesitate. Her sister's death is clearly a sore spot, and with someone as unstable as Kendall Cooper, I have to tread carefully. "I know what it's like to lose someone. In grief, I know people can do a lot of irrational things. I don't want to judge you for that. I want to help you, Kendall."

Kendall's gaze softens a bit—not much, but a bit. She looks a little less like she wants to murder me.

"How would you help me?" she asks.

"We could get you into witness protection," I say. "Give you a different name, dye your hair, make you a different person. Then we could use the information you have to arrest your parents. You could avoid jail and help bring down the Coopers."

Kendall's expression changes, and I realize that she's figured out my plan. I think she realizes I'm not going to hurt her. She holsters her gun. That's when I notice the bomb taped to the stands above. It's only about one square foot, but I know it is more than enough to kill a couple dozen people up in the stands.

"No," she says, turning to look up at the bomb on the underside of the stands, her expression twisted as if she is looking at something she despises. "I know you mean well, Danielle, but you need to get out of here before this place blows."

I work up the courage to take a step closer to her.

"Kendall," I say. "You don't have to do this. Those people up there don't deserve this. Those are *innocent people*. Just like you didn't deserve what your parents did to you when you were a little girl, those people up there don't deserve to die."

Kendall turns to me, her gaze cold and hard, like it was when I confronted her outside the nightclub just last night.

"You're wrong," she says and jabs a finger up to the stands above her so forcefully I jump. "*Those people* up there are my parents. *Those* are the people who killed Natalie and so many others. They deserve to die more than anyone else in the world."

I realize my mouth has fallen slightly open, but no words are coming out of it. How does she know her parents are up there? Has she been tracking them? Has all of this not only been a response to her sister's death but a plot to kill her parents?

"Is that why you went back to crime?" I ask, my voice sounding small. I try to remember I'm talking to a fifteen-year-old, but it hardly helps. "To get revenge on your parents?"

Kendall looks away. "All they ever wanted was to be feared," she says. "They wanted to make a name for themselves, so everyone would know the role they played in the Clan. But...I figured if I could outdo them, if I could get people to fear me more than them, it would ruin them. It would be more than enough revenge. I didn't know where they were until recently. Otherwise, this would have been my plan from the beginning." My heart aches as she unfolds her plan for me. All she wanted to do was avenge her sister. And she always felt like she had to do it alone. It's saddening, and horrifying all at once.

"But Kendall," I say. "You could have come to the police. You could have just turned them in."

"If I had gone to the police, I would have been arrested," she says, her tone as cold as her stare. "And my parents might be horrible, but they're not stupid. The police wouldn't have caught them."

Then I say something that without a doubt risks my life farther than I ever have before, but it's the only thing that will get through to Kendall Cooper in this moment.

"Natalie wouldn't have wanted this. You know, she wouldn't have wanted you to do this."

Kendall looks at me, and I swear I have never seen a kid look so old. Her voice cracks when she speaks. "This is all I know how to do."

That's when a chorus of yelling and footsteps erupts behind me. Somewhere in the chaos, I make out the word "police." Before I have time to register what is about to happen, a gunshot rings out, and Kendall Cooper falls to the ground.

CHAPTER THIRTY-ONE

KENDALL

I'm in a room with black walls, ceilings, and floors. A black cube, more like. I study it in awe for a moment before I realize it's not a room at all. I'm just surrounded by darkness. Fog hovers over the ground, and the cloud comes up to my waist. My mind is drowsy, and I can't think straight. I wonder if I've been drugged. This should worry me, right? But I'm so tired, and my mind is too slow, I can't even process my thoughts. I begin to walk through the cloud. I walk through the darkness. My tentative footsteps echo through the large open space.

I don't know how long I've been walking. Maybe minutes. Maybe hours. It feels more like my legs are floating than I'm physically taking steps. I see something in the distance. I begin to float toward it. It looks like the silhouette of a person. When I finally reach them and my fuzzy mind registers who it is, my heart stops.

"Nat?" My voice is raspy and barely above a whisper. My sister turns to me, and the second we make eye contact, I'm sitting down. On my bed. I'm twelve years old. It must be close to two in the morning, but sleep had never really been one of my strong points. Too many nightmares. The people I killed, staring me back in the face. I remember now. This is the night before Natalie's death.

"The plan is flawless," Natalie whispers, and I feel like I've been pulled out of a dream. I jump.

"Huh? What?" I stutter, still shaken.

"Our plan is flawless," Natalie repeats, just as she did the first time. She looks up at me. "But I promise you, there are risks. This is more dangerous than any other assignment we've ever had. Do you understand?"

"Yes," I say authoritatively. "This is the only way—" My voice catches, and it feels as if there's something stuck in my throat. "This is the only way—" I try again but stop in the same place. The full sentence is: This is the only way we will ever be happy. But I remember something. Something is wrong.

"No," I say. My voice is strong, as if I'm defying someone, but I'm not sure who. "*No*. We already went through with the plan. It went bad. You *died*." I make eye contact with her. I can't explain how I know this. The plan is tomorrow, but it's as if I have already lived it. "I'm never happy again."

Natalie just smiles at me. "You're so brave," she says, just as she did on that night. I stand up and look at my old room. Panic begins to set in as I start to remember. As I remember things that haven't happened to me yet. Things, people, places, feelings, I don't know.

"No," I say again. "I don't live here anymore. I left! We left!" I am practically screaming now, and I try to catch my breath. What's happening? "And—and..." I feel like I'm suffocating. Am I dying? I fall to the ground, and it's as if I'm watching a movie of my own life.

I see Natalie's death. I see me running through the woods, away from my old life. Away from Natalie. I see myself living on the streets. I see myself hungrier than I've ever been in my life. I see myself stealing food. I see myself finding Milo. I see myself meeting Juan. Walking into a cabin in the woods. I see myself in Fort Knox. Laughing with Cecelia. The bank robbery. Eduardo getting shot. Getting kicked out of the gang. The clips of my life are flashing through my mind so fast I can barely process them. Then I see myself stepping on that twig in my dream. I see myself in the basketball stadium. I see that cop, Danielle. I see police officers with automatic weapons running in behind her. I see one of them aimed at me. It fires.

My eyes open, and I sit up with a gasp. I'm in a bed. A white *hospital* bed. The walls are white, and on the left side of my bed are three chairs. Various tubes and wires are connected to me, and beeping machines surround me. I'm in a hospital. And I. Remember. Everything.

"No," I say, quietly at first. "No. No! No! NO!" I begin to scream and thrash in my bed. My stomach is screaming with pain, and I pull at the tubes and wires, leaving needles and bits of plastic in my body, but I don't care. I don't feel them. I don't feel the bullet hole in my stomach. All I feel is the crippling pain inside of me, and all I want to do is scream it out. I can feel tears pouring out of my eyes by the bucketful, and I still don't care. This is the first time I've cried since Natalie died. I feel a breathing tube up my nostrils, and I yank it out. One of the machines begins to beep faster. I try to get out of the bed, but a single handcuff on my right wrist connecting me to the bed keeps me down. I just keep screaming. People in lab coats swarm in, and I feel their hands on me, attempting to hold me down. I don't even try to compose myself at the sight of them, because standing in front of me is the big, ugly truth. I. Failed.

Not only did I just as well as kill my sister, but I failed in my one chance to avenge her. I let that goddamn cop get the better of me, and now I will never be able to get justice for my sister. Even if I was the cause of her death. I am everything Ma'am and Sir said and worse. I am a monster. I am stupid. And pathetic. And in the battle against my parents, I realize now, I will never win.

I feel a sharp jab to my neck, and all the fight drains out of me. The world begins to fade away, and I succumb to the darkness.

~

When I wake up this time, I already know where I am. I already know what has happened. More than anything, I wish I could forget it. The second I get out of the hospital, I'll be sent to prison, or even worse. The adrenaline and anger have been knocked out of me, I'm guessing by the drugs, so I can't sit up, or even begin to stand up and walk on my own. That means that I am completely confined to the hospital until I can function again. There's no point in contemplating an escape plan when even the newborns in the maternity ward could take me in my current state.

It's almost funny. All my life, I've thought of myself as a fighter. I've always tried to fight back against the people, or those in power, that have hurt me. My parents. The Clan. The gang. The police. The law. The government. Even if I have already lost, I keep finding new ways to fight. And win.

But here I am, handcuffed to a hospital bed with a bullet in my stomach, utterly and completely defeated.

CHAPTER THIRTY-TWO

DANIELLE

I sit in the hospital waiting room, bouncing my leg up and down, matching the rhythm of my heart. My pulse pounds in my temple, and I feel sick to my stomach. Everything has gone so wrong. I close my eyes, hoping to get some relief, but all I see are the flashing lights of the ambulance that took Kendall Cooper to the hospital. When I saw those lights, I knew my life was over.

Only no one but myself has said that. I open my eyes. I betrayed my oath, I attempted to help a criminal, and somehow, I got caught in the act. Yet no one has slapped a pair of handcuffs on my wrists and read me my rights. This small relief only stirs up more questions in my mind. Why? And more importantly, how? Normal police protocol would be to arrest me on the spot, the second Cooper was down. I would be considered an active threat against the law. But I'm sitting in the waiting room of a public hospital, alone. Like any normal, *free* person would. There have to be some other forces at play here.

The door of the waiting room swings open, and I stand up. This must be them. This must be the feds coming to arrest me, or at the very least relieve me of duty. It surprises me that I'm almost eager to face them. I betrayed everything a good cop stands for. I deserve this. I made a choice. Kendall Cooper or my oath, and I managed to fail both of them. Yes. I deserve this.

However, it isn't a federal officer who walks in but Nicki. Her face looks like it has aged five years, and more than that, she has the look every half-decent criminal I've arrested has had in their eyes: guilt. My heart crawls up into my throat as I realize this. What could Nicki have done to make her look like she's the criminal instead of me?

I walk up to her. "What is it?" I ask. Her eyes scan the waiting room, and they land on an elderly couple sitting in the corner, reading the paper.

"Could we talk somewhere private?" Nicki asks tentatively.

"Sure," I say, a little more than slightly nervous at Nicki's demeanor. She takes my arm and pulls me down the hallway and into the janitor's closet. She isn't exactly gentle about it, so I'm guessing she's mad. Mops and cleaning supplies line the walls, and I instinctively check for security cameras. There are none. This is the perfect place to talk in secret.

"So what happened tonight?" I ask firmly. The familiar expression of guilt and a look of anger battle to take over Nicki's face as she hesitates to answer the question. This does not put me at ease.

"I called the feds," she says quickly. I barely catch it, and shock overtakes my body.

"What?" I ask. Did I hear that right? Did my best friend really just admit to betraying me? Did she really just admit to turning me in? I think of the life I wanted. To have a future with Jason, maybe have kids someday. All of that stripped away by my best friend. "What?!" My tone is more forceful the second time.

Nicki looks around, as if the walls themselves have ears. "Shhhh!" she urges. "It's not like that, I promise!"

"Really?" I say, folding my arms over my chest. "Because it *sounds* like you just turned me in."

"Please just listen," she says. I wait for her to speak, not having anything to say until I hear her side of it. "When you went in, when you walked out of the car, it was like I was watching you leave me. Like permanently. I know what the Mors Clan is capable of. I've seen it. The thought of you being alone with one of them..." She trails off for a moment. I open my mouth to object, but she cuts me off before I can say anything. "I thought I was going to lose you. Dani, you're my best friend; I couldn't just let you die."

"So you turned me in?" I say, feeling my face get hot. I don't think I've ever been angry at Nicki before, not like this. "You ruined my life to prevent my death?!"

"No," Nicki says, her voice oddly calm for the situation. "I didn't turn you in. I lied to the station to get back up."

This surprises me. For a moment, I let myself feel some relief. I'm not going to prison.

"What did you tell them?" I ask.

"I said that the bug we put on the gang member's shoe was out of range, and by the time we heard that Cooper was going to the stadium, there wasn't enough time to assemble a squad. I said that you went in to try to stall her long enough for backup." A mixture of anger and relief washes over me. Even though I'm not going to jail, Nicki still betrayed me. She still went against our friendship and partnership. Years worth of trust...gone. But are they really gone? I try to put myself in her shoes. If I thought that she was about to die, who knows what I would have done to try and save her. Would I have called for backup against her will if I thought her life depended on it?

I really don't want to think about that. I don't want to see the other side of this, because if it's even possible, it makes this whole situation even more complicated.

Finally, I say, "Thanks. It means a lot that you didn't turn me in."

Nicki gives me a half-hearted smile. "I don't even think I could." She pauses, and her expression is more serious. "Are we going to be OK?"

I bite my lip and consider the question for a moment. Through all this I'm going to need Nicki. I don't think I can afford to be angry at her with all that I have on my plate.

"I think we will be," I say, my tone a bit softer than before. I unfold my arms and try to resume my normal composure. "So what's our next move? Just continue the case like nothing happened? How are we supposed to do interrogations in a hospital?"

"I'm not sure," Nicki says. "Only there's one more thing. After you left, I spoke with Agent Danvers. She caught Cooper's parents at the stadium after you relayed what Kendall Cooper told you to her." My heart skips a beat. I smile. Once Agent Danvers arrived on the scene, I told her the whereabouts of Rebecca and Tristan Cooper, and now they are no longer a threat to this world. Even if I have failed to help Kendall Cooper, this is one good thing that came out of tonight. "But she needs you to question Kendall Cooper and get evidence against them. She believes that with Cooper's testimony, they would be eligible for the death penalty or at least life in solitary confinement. So as of right now, we are to treat her as a witness and not a criminal."

The thought of talking to Kendall Cooper again makes my stomach churn. She can't be happy about what happened today. According to her perspective and the official report, I was just there to stall her until a squad arrived to capture her. I feel sick thinking about it. Did I cause her death?

"We don't even know if she's alive or capable of talking. Last I saw her, she was getting rushed into surgery," I say. "And even if she is, she won't want to talk to me."

Nicki shrugs. "Well, you'll have to think of something, because Agent Danvers was very specific about *you* being the one to talk to her. She really seems to have taken a liking to you."

I nod. I can't ignore my duty. "If she's alive, I'll figure something out." We walk out of the closet and back into the waiting room, where a woman in a long white lab coat has her back to us, talking to the person at the desk. When we walk in, she turns and walks toward us.

"Hello," she says in a friendly yet tired voice. "I'm Dr. Boone. I assume you're the detective on Kendall Cooper's case?"

My body tenses with anticipation, and I try not to let it register on my face. "Yes," I say. "I was hoping to speak with her as soon as possible." I pause. "That is...if it *is* possible."

"Well, visiting hours are over, but you can come back in the morning," she says. "Kendall Cooper is in stable condition for now." Relief washes over me, and the doctor walks back through the doors to the hallway. I walk with Nicki to the elevator. I know I've got a hell of a day ahead of me tomorrow, but for now I let myself bask in relief. Kendall Cooper is alive.

CHAPTER THIRTY-THREE

KENDALL

It's the next morning, I think. I can only tell because the sun is shining through the window of my room; otherwise, I would have been sure that it was midnight. I'm exhausted. Even small things like sitting up and trying to eat with a spoon are incredibly painful and tiring. I can't tell if it's from the bullet hole in me or from my current mental state. Does it matter? Just digesting my food is like hell. The truth is that I will never get out of my prison sentence. I can only imagine the mountain of evidence against me, as I made no attempt to hide my identity as a criminal. Not to mention, I can't even walk, much less try to escape.

I shift my weight, and a stabbing pain in my stomach makes me stop. I grit my teeth to keep from crying out. I won't give them the satisfaction of hearing me whimper like a hurt puppy. I wonder if the nurses here are laughing at me. Girl who thought she could take over the world, shot and wounded, unable to move without crying out. I bite down on my lip so hard that it bleeds. I hate this. I hate it all so much. I was supposed to be dead by now. Death would be so much better than this.

"Kendall?" the woman sitting next to my bed says in her gentle, tentative voice. I almost forgot she was there. The shrink they set up for me. She's an older woman, about five feet tall, and always hunched over. She strikes me as the type of woman who is afraid of her own shadow.

"Huh?" I say, not even remotely interested in what she has to say.

"I asked about your sister's death," she prompts. I feel like I have been punched in the gut. Another reminder of my failure. Of how I got Natalie killed. It takes physical effort to keep my expression neutral. I have to remind myself that this woman is a therapist for prisoners. Her job is to break me.

"What about it?" I ask.

"Well, it seems to be a sore subject for you," the woman says. Her expression is full of pity, and I have to sit on my hands to keep myself from strangling her. It hurts, but killing her will only get me in deeper trouble. I have to keep a cool head until I figure out what my angle will be for my trial. Playing innocent wouldn't work very well if I strangled this woman in the hospital.

"I mean, I guess," I say, trying to keep my answers as neutral as possible.

"Do you want to tell me what happened?" she asks softly.

"No," I say. She looks at me, waiting for me to say more, but I don't open my mouth.

She sighs. "You know, we are going to make very little progress if you can't open up to me. I can't treat someone who doesn't want to be treated."

I don't respond. I really want to kill her. I want to kill her more than I've wanted to kill anyone in my entire life. Except my parents. My anger at her cools a bit. Sir and Ma'am are alive and well and are going to get away because *I* failed. I have never wanted to kill anyone more than them. I have to remember that. If I ever get out of here, killing them will be the first thing I do. I will make sure their deaths are slow and brutal, and I will make sure they feel every single wound until the moment they take their last breath. Until I remember that I can't. I will never be able to kill my parents.

I punch the buzzer next to my bed that the nurse told me is only to be used in emergencies.

"Medical emergency!" I holler. "Medical emergency!" My voice is still hoarse from last night, and the expanding and contracting of my stomach sends pain shooting up my ribs, but as long as it gets this woman away from me, I don't care.

The woman has her jaw on the floor when one of my nurses, a larger woman with hair dyed bright red, comes in. The therapist argues with her, but the nurse still ushers her out of the room. After the incident last night, I doubt she wants to take any chances.

I hear something that sounds like, "In all my years," and the therapist leaves. However, that isn't the end of it. I hear another woman's voice outside, and it sounds familiar. I can't quite place it, but I feel like I know her. I can't make out the words that she's saying, and I hear footsteps coming toward me.

In walks Danielle Toole, the cop who tricked me. The cop who nearly got me killed. The stupid, manipulative bitch who is the reason I failed. Without even thinking, I grab a mug filled to the brim with cold coffee from this morning and throw it at her. Her eyes grow wide, and she dodges it. It hits the wall and shatters. Brown liquid explodes from it and stains the wall. She staggers back and looks at me, her expression still shocked. So much for my innocent plea.

I don't have anything else to throw at her, and I'm handcuffed to the bed, so there's really nothing else I can do but glare daggers at her. This seems to have no effect on her. She composes herself and sits down calmly in the chair next to my bed, the same one that the therapist lady sat in. I have no idea what to say to her that won't start with a death threat, so we just hold eye contact for a long time before she speaks.

She speaks in a calm, authoritative voice. "I thought you would like to know that with the information you gave us last night, we were able to catch your parents in the basketball stadium. Rebecca and Tristan Cooper are in custody." Silence. My parents are in custody. My parents are in custody. I repeat the sentence over and over in my head, not believing it until I finally say it out loud.

"My parents are in custody," I say. I don't know whether to laugh or cry about all of it. My parents' life plan failed. They are in police custody because of me. But it also means that I failed. I won't be able to kill them when they're in custody. But was my goal ever really to kill them? Wasn't it originally just to ruin them? Haven't I done that? It doesn't feel like a win. But it doesn't feel like a loss either.

"Yes," Danielle says. "However, as you've said, they *are* good at covering their tracks. We were only able to link them to a small number of crimes as opposed to all the ones we suspect they have committed." My heart sinks. I wonder how many a "small number" is in Toole's stupid mind. Probably not enough to give them twenty years. Probably just a couple counts of shoplifting to feed themselves when money was tight. I allow a look of absolute disgust to take over my face.

"You're pathetic," I say, letting every bit of resentment I have for the woman in front of me leak into my voice. "You can't get even a shred of evidence to convict them! You are a pathetic whore who has never cared about anyone but herself! You know, if you were half decent at your job, my parents would be on their way to a fucking life sentence!" I would say more, but even yelling hurts, and I have to stop. I hope this was at least enough to offend her. However, her expression is defensive.

"I tried to help you last night!" she says, lowering her voice.

"Sure!" I yell. My stomach screams with pain, but I ignore it. "Sure you did! Of course someone like you would try to help someone like me! If you thought I would fall for the 'I still want to help you' act, you're even dumber than I thought you were!"

Danielle looks around and leans in to me, closer than I would have if I was her.

"Between you and me," she says, "I really didn't plan for the squad to come in. I swear." She pauses, as if unsure if she should speak again. "I'm sorry." I'm taken aback by this. She actually sounds sincere, but she sounded sincere at the basketball stadium, and look how that turned out. But if she really wants to help me, she won't be able to do it if I keep shutting her down. And even if she is really lying, giving the illusion of trust will give me an advantage. Either way, acting like I trust her will benefit me.

I sit up a little straighter. "Fine. But what are you doing here?" I ask. "What do you need from me?"

She pulls out her phone, and I see a red recording button surrounded by plain black on the screen. "I need your testimony about what your parents did to you," she says. My immediate reaction is hell no. I would rather die than relive the horrors of my childhood. Danielle sees my expression and speaks before I have an opportunity to decline.

"I know it will be hard for you, but this is the only way to get them into solitary confinement so they can never hurt anyone the way they hurt you. Maybe even the death sentence if we're lucky." The death sentence. Now that has my attention. Reliving my trauma to have a chance at killing my parents. I weigh my options. If I tell Danielle all of the things that have happened in my life, she could take advantage of the information and use it against me. Will I let the possibility of my parents' death lead to my demise? Or is that Danielle's plan? Use what she knows drives me to get information to use against me. No. I will not be used by her again.

Danielle clearly senses my hesitancy and speaks in a kind, soft voice. "Kendall, do you know why I was so driven to help you?" I think about it for a moment. I'd guessed it was a lie that she wanted to help me at all, but I'd never really thought about what could have motivated her had it actually been true. I shake my head. Danielle pauses before she speaks again, hesitating herself. "Just a few months before I was put on your case, I lost my sister." She pauses again, as if expecting a reaction, but I don't give her one. If she knew about Natalie, she knows that my sister died too. I begin to let my guard down a bit. Maybe Danielle is really telling the truth. "She...um...was a very special person in my life. The person who inspired me to become a detective, actually." Her voice is tight and strained, as if she is far away. She pauses again, and a deep sorrow comes over her face. "I got married without her at the ceremony. I spent my entire wedding day and every day since then that I was supposed to be happy just thinking about how she wasn't there. My sister is gone, and nothing will bring her back to enjoy those moments with me." She pauses, and her expression wavers, as if she is about to cry. She takes a breath, composes herself, and continues. "Then I was put on your case, and as I learned more and more about you, you became less of a suspect to me and more of...well, a person. When I realized that what you were doing was out of grief—and for a sister, no less—I knew I couldn't just let you get arrested. I knew I had to help you."

There is a long silence between us. I want to believe that everything she just told me was a lie. I want to believe that she is just trying to manipulate me into helping her again. But everything about it seemed so real. So genuine. And some stupid part of me thinks back to Juan. How I thought he was just a jerk. Another tool in the gang. And he turned out to have his reasons for being a jerk. He turned into my closest ally after I was kicked out of the gang. The same stupid part of me wants to believe her. I want to believe that like Juan, there's more to her than meets the eye.

"Fine," I say, finally accepting her as someone trustworthy. "I will help you."

CHAPTER THIRTY-FOUR

DANIELLE

Kendall Cooper's report of her parents' abuse and other crimes that she can remember takes ten hours to go over. Ten hours. By the time she's done and I have taken all of the recordings and notes I can, we are both exhausted. She receives her lunch, and I step out of the room, contemplating what I just heard. This information has only made me more sympathetic to her cause, which is horrible, because it's only a reminder of how I failed her. I wish there was some way that I could help her. But that opportunity has passed me by.

It's strange how guilty I feel about this. Usually I get a sense of pride at catching a criminal. It means I did my job, and I did it successfully. But now...I don't know. Can I even continue with detective work knowing that I've sided with a criminal? I have allowed myself to get so attached to this case; will I be able to detach myself from cases in the future? I'm not sure.

I let my head rest against the wall of the hallway. Across the hall from me is the closed door to Kendall Cooper's room. It occurs to me how similar this feels to the day Amanda died. After she died, the ambulance brought her body back to the hospital. I didn't have anywhere that I could go, so they brought me too. A nurse wrapped me in a blanket and told me that the police were here, and I could talk to them whenever I was ready. That hospital was eerily similar to this one. Not only that, but I have that same sinking feeling. The feeling that someone I care about is slipping out of my grasp, and moreover, that it is all my fault. I had problems before my sister's death, but looking back, everything seems so easy. Jason had proposed to me a few months ago, I had been planning the wedding, we had bought a house, I had a well-paying job I was happy in, the best sister I could ever ask for by my side, and now all of it has fallen apart. All of my problems started in a hospital. Is this the start of another rollercoaster to hell, or is this bringing my problems full circle? Can I *end* all of my problems in this hospital?

"Dani!" I hear a familiar voice from behind me. I smile. Jason. I turn and see that he's holding a plastic bag in his hand. He smiles back at me and holds the bag up. "I brought lunch."

~

The nurses let us use their break room, so that's where we eat lunch. I haven't eaten anything since last night, so the food Jason brought is a welcome treat. I scarf the food down in minutes and am nowhere near full. Jason is still munching on his sandwich. As he eats, I gaze into his soft brown eyes. He really is the perfect husband, isn't he?

Jason catches my gaze and gives me a warm smile. He sits up a little straighter. "Pretty crazy last night," he says, wiping his mouth. Clearly he is expecting me to elaborate on what happened.

Guilt gnaws at me and makes the food that is beginning to settle in my stomach turn sour. I hadn't gotten a chance to talk to Jason last night. I had just texted him that I made it home and ended up falling asleep on the couch before he had gotten back from work. He was at the basketball stadium, cleaning up the mess I made. There's no way I can hide the truth from him. I know that he will understand what I did more than anyone else in the world.

I look around the room, and only when I'm sure that there are no cameras do I begin to speak. "I actually need to talk to you about that," I confess.

Jason's eyes leap up from his plate to me. His worried expression only makes me feel more guilty. "What is it?"

I take a deep breath. "The police report from last night is inaccurate," I begin. "It... I... I went into that basketball stadium to try to talk Cooper out of the bomb, like the report said, but Nicki lied about the bug on the gang member's shoe being out of range." The words practically fall out of my mouth. Jason arches his eyebrows in confusion.

"What?" he says in disbelief. And just like that, the guilt returns. I have been such a basket case lately. He has had to put up with so much of my crap in these past few months, and now this. I hate myself for being so needy with him, and I hate that I have made him feel my pain.

I sigh. "I was going to try to get her into witness protection, so we could catch her parents and put an end to the Mors Clan. Believe me, Jason, when I say that the girl in that hospital bed does not deserve to go to prison." I point in the direction of Kendall's room then look back at Jason. He just stares at me in shock. However, there's something else. He's putting his hand to his chin, the way he always does when he's thinking deeply about something. I lower my gaze. "You think I'm crazy, don't you?"

There is a terrifying moment of silence between us that I'm convinced means that he does. Thankfully, the moment passes, and he begins to speak. "Of course I don't," he says, looking back up at me with his soft, caring eyes. "I've always trusted your judgment, Dani. You just have to remember that you're not in this alone." He pauses. "You could have told me sooner. I would have helped you."

I nod sorrowfully. This is the best I could have hoped for this to go, but it still doesn't feel right. Jason feels betrayed, and I can't take back my actions.

"I'm sorry," I say. "It just all happened so fast, and by the time I got around to thinking about telling you, it was—"

"Don't be sorry," he says, cutting me off. He pauses before he speaks again. "Do you remember the Beatrice Cole case?" I nod. It was a few years ago, back when I first became a detective and started dating Jason. Beatrice Cole, a mother stabbed to death in her home. I remember the whole thing like it was yesterday. "I don't know if I ever told you, but the day you solved that case was the day I fell in love with you." I feel myself blush and allow a smile to take over my face, and Jason continues. "Everyone thought that the woman's ex-husband was the murderer. He didn't have an alibi, he had motive, and even though we didn't have any physical evidence to convict him, he had threatened Beatrice's life before, and everyone on the case was sure that it was him. But not you. Somehow, you *knew* that her current husband was the killer. So you marched your rookie ass down to their house and bluffed your way through the interrogation until you got him to confess. I was shocked when I went into work the next day and heard you had arrested him yourself." I chuckle a bit, reliving the memory. He smiles. "I fell in love with you because I know that no matter what, you will do what you believe is right." He moves his chair closer to me. "And right now, what do you think that is?"

I hesitate. There are a number of things that I could do to help Cooper, given her background. I could claim that she was brainwashed, which to a certain extent is true, which is likely to land her in an asylum rather than juvenile detention. But that's the best-case scenario, and it doesn't quite sit right with me. Cooper deserves a second chance, but I know that there is no possible way I can give that to her.

"I'm really not sure," I finally answer.

"Well, no matter what you do," he says, and kisses me on the cheek, "I'll always love you."

CHAPTER THIRTY-FIVE

KENDALL

I walk slowly from one end of the small recovery room to the other. The exercise isn't tiring, but it is painful, and after it's over, I lean against the wall. It has been a week since I was shot, and the doctors say I *should* make a full recovery. I've been progressing nicely, or so they say, and I'm not exactly sure when they will put me in jail to await my trial. I'm guessing it will be once I'm able to actually walk from my cell to my trial, which if I'm predicting right, is soon. They've read my rights more times than I can count, and since there is no one to bail me out until my trial, I'm pretty much stuck here until my state-provided attorney meets with me to discuss my story for the trial. Danielle hasn't come to ask me any more questions, so I assume that she has no further use for me. I doubt I'll ever see her again, so there goes my one potential ally. They've been very aggressive in my recovery, and I can tell the staff are eager to get me out of the hospital. It's not like I could hurt them or anything. Walking the width of the recovery room and back is a workout for me now, and I have a police officer following me around everywhere with a taser, gun, pepper spray, etc. I could probably take the cop out if I was at full strength and could move the way I used to, but that really wouldn't do me much good since there is a police station less than five minutes away, and the nurses have warned me repeatedly that more officers will be here in minutes if I do anything sketchy. Fan-fucking-tastic.

"Great job, Kendall," the physical therapist says, smiling at me. I think her name is Susan or Suzie or something. I only remember because she's one of the few people here that treats me like a normal person. I'm sure she knows about the things I've done, but it's like she interacts with people like me every day.

"Your recovery has been impressive. Most patients at this stage are still learning to stand," she says.

"Yeah, well, your team hasn't exactly been shy about rushing the recovery process," I retort. By her team, I'm referring to the hospital staff who have been helping me since I got shot. Or more like forced to help me.

Susan looks around and sees my control officer across the room, in the doorway, playing on his phone. Typical.

"Between you and me," Susan begins, lowering her voice substantially, "the FBI wants you out of here as soon as possible. They have tried to pull you out several times, but you can only speed up a recovery so much. You're getting released tomorrow."

My heart sinks. I knew this was going to happen. I knew that I was going to be released, I knew I was going to be thrown in prison, and I knew there was no escaping my fate. But still, when Susan tells me, it feels like I'm realizing it all for the first time. Maybe her saying it out loud makes it more real.

I can feel myself deflate. I have been so focused on my failure and my injury, I've hardly thought about going to prison. I thought I had accepted it. Prison really never seemed so bad. Free food. Free bedding. People to entertain me and beat up if I ever felt the need to. I would never go hungry or worry about freezing to death if it got too cold, and more than that, it would keep me away from any and all reminders of Natalie and how I failed her in every way I could. Then why don't I want to go? What could possibly be tying me to the outside world?

I don't have time to figure it out before Susan's watch beeps, signaling that my physical therapy session is over. She gives me a reassuring smile, which doesn't help anything, and my officer grabs my arm and pulls me into the wheelchair that is waiting for me in the hall. He secures the handcuff around my right wrist and puts the other one around the arm of the wheelchair. He pushes me down the hall to my room, and when I get there, I see the sky outside is dark. Stars dot it, and I can see the Big Dipper.

It's midnight. I'm in my old bed. Natalie is lying in her bed across the room. I'm nine years old. I can't sleep.

"Nat," I whisper, knowing she isn't asleep. She sits up.

"What is it?" she asks.

"I can't sleep," I say. I don't have to go into detail about the nightmares. She knows. She always knows.

"Me either," she says, and to my surprise she stands up and walks toward the bedroom window. "Come on."

I stand up and follow her. "Where are we going?" I ask.

"You'll see," she says. She quietly opens the window and climbs out. I'm surprised by this, but I trust Natalie, so I follow her out onto the roof of our old house. She climbs to the top of the roof near the chimney, not even showing a hint of fear. I copy her, and we sit next to each other on top of the roof. I hold on to the top, afraid I might fall, though I don't tell her. Crickets chirp in the woods around us, and for a while we just sit there.

She points up at the sky. "Look," she says. "Right there, that group of stars that looks kind of like a spoon?" I look up, and it takes me a minute, but finally I make out the outline of a sort of ladle in the sky. My mouth drops open. I'd never seen a constellation before.

"Oh my gosh," I whisper, staring in awe at the group of stars. I had no idea that the sky itself could make something so beautiful.

"That's the Big Dipper," she says and begins pointing out other constellations to me in the sky. All my anxiety about the nightmares fades away as I look up at the stars and feel Natalie at my side. In that moment, maybe for the first time in my life, I could say that everything was perfect.

I look up at the Big Dipper now. Five years later. Natalie is gone, but the stars haven't changed. The officer helps me into bed and then handcuffs me to it, like he's trying to remind me that I'm still a prisoner.

For some stupid reason this makes me want to cry. The idea of going to prison makes me want to bawl like a little baby. I bite the inside of my cheek as hard as I can to keep myself from crying. My control officer is still here, and I cannot cry in front of him. I'm sure he already thinks I'm pathetic enough as it is.

However, to my luck, his phone rings, and he takes the call outside. I still don't allow myself to cry, but it lets me relax a bit. It doesn't last long, since he walks back in after about a minute, looking angry.

"Detective Toole is coming to speak with you," he says, then leaves.

CHAPTER THIRTY-SIX

DANIELLE

I walk into Kendall Cooper's room, and her expression is nothing short of surprised. I told the station that I had some follow-up questions for her, which was a lie. She's getting released from the hospital tomorrow morning, and I don't know, I guess I wanted to see her again before the only way I'll be able to talk to her is from the other side of prison glass. To be honest, I'm not even sure what I'm doing here.

"I thought you were done with me," Kendall says. I close the door to her room, so that it's just the two of us.

"Honestly," I say, "I did too." Kendall sits up a little straighter.

"Then what are you doing here?" she asks.

I hesitate. "I just wanted to see you one more time, I guess," I half-lie. Kendall seems to take notice of my uncertainty but doesn't say anything about it.

"Well, you've seen me," she says, then pauses and looks out the window as if deep in thought. "You were telling the truth, weren't you? About your sister. You were really trying to help me." She looks back at me. "Otherwise, you wouldn't have come back."

It shouldn't really surprise me that she thought I was lying. I doubt she can even count how many times she's been lied to in her life. But it does surprise me, and I open my mouth, trying to find the right words. It takes a minute to finally get what I want to say out of my mouth.

"Of course I was telling the truth," I say. I know it isn't much, but I hope it means something to her. Kendall seems to be debating something in her mind, and finally her expression settles. I wait for her to speak.

"Do you know that what happened the night I left the Clan..." She pauses. "It was my fault." This catches me off guard.

"What do you mean?" I ask.

"Nat..." Her voice cracks, like it did that night at the stadium, and she inhales shakily. "Nat and I were running through the woods, trying to escape Ma'am and Sir, but I stepped on a twig. I gave us away, and that's how they knew where to shoot." I notice tears trickling down her face, but I don't say anything. She pauses to wipe them from her face, and her expression hardens. "It was my fault. I deserve this." I stare at her for a moment, realizing why exactly I was so drawn to her. Not just her sister's death, but her reaction to it. I never realized just how alike we are.

"Sometimes, you get into tough situations, and bad things happen," I say. "Things that cost you a lot. But that doesn't mean it was your fault." I pause and take a breath. I speak slowly. "It wasn't your fault." I realize the weight of my words, as I repeat them to myself in my head. *It wasn't your fault.* I feel a few tears slide down my own cheeks. I can't even begin to discern my emotions at the moment, but it feels like an elephant has just been lifted off of my shoulders. "I used to think that the world was divided into black and white. It's how I had to think, I was a detective, I had to arrest people, so I had to pretend they were all bad guys. But that's not true. There's no such thing as black and white, good and bad." I pause and look at her. We lock eyes, and I realize that for the first time in a long time, I feel...OK. "You taught me that. Whether you realized it or not."

She lets out a sigh that nearly resembles a laugh. "I'm not sure why I'm so open with you. I guess when you know you're about to spend the rest of your life in a cell, you know there's nothing to lose."

"Kendall," I begin, trying to use a calming tone until I realize I don't know what to say. Looking at her now, I realize I don't want her life to be ruined. I want her to find some solace, some semblance of peace. After a moment, the words finally come to me. "What makes you happy?" She looks out the window again, and for a long time, she doesn't speak. She looks down at her lap and then back out the window.

"The woods," she says, so quietly I can barely hear it. "My family would move around a lot, but it was almost always somewhere near the woods." She pauses, and I see tears shining in her eyes, reflecting the moonlight. "When things got bad, Natalie would always take me into the woods. Out of the house. It was like an escape." A single tear escapes her right eye, and she wipes it away. "I guess, whenever I go into the woods now, it just makes me feel closer to her." She pauses again and looks down at her lap. "But there aren't any woods in prison...so..." She trails off before she collects herself. "That's a pretty shitty reason not to want to go to prison, right?" I don't answer but look out the window with her, noticing she's looking at the tree line in the distance. I internally sigh. I know if she goes to prison, she will never be happy again. I feel the stalemate of the situation once again settle around me. There's nothing I can do to help her. All I've done is make myself feel worse and more helpless than ever. That is until a plan hatches in my mind. Again, it is dangerous, but I know I need to do it. My first plan to help her might have failed, but this one won't. I know because this time I'm sure. I'm sure that this is the right thing to do. I'm sure that this is what I need to do.

"Kendall," I say, moving closer to her. "I need you to listen to me very carefully." My tone is authoritative, but my voice is hushed. Kendall senses that I'm about to tell her something important, and the tears fade as she listens. "You are two stories up in this hospital. There is a fire escape outside your window."

"What are you—" she begins curiously, but I cut her off.

"Just listen," I say. "I am going to drop my phone. There is a whole nest of bobby pins holding up my bun. When I bend down to pick my phone up, grab one of them. Trust me. I know crime scenes, and for this to work, we need to play it out exactly like it was really an accident." Kendall seems to have figured out what I'm telling her to do, and her face brightens. "Stick the bobby pin in the lock of your handcuffs, turn away, then turn back. The handcuffs will unlock, and you are going to go out the window and not look back. Do you understand?"

Kendall looks shocked and relieved, but she only nods. "Thank you," she says, her voice sounding as if she is lost in a dream.

"No," I say. "Thank *you*." Before she can say another word, I fumble with my phone, and it drops to the ground. I bend down to pick it up and feel the slight tug at my bun that I know I would have missed if I wasn't specifically feeling for it. I stand back up and look at the girl who has changed me in so many ways, one last time. She gives me a grateful nod, and I nod back. "I never saw anything." I turn my back and walk out of the room knowing that it will be the last time I ever see Kendall Cooper.

TWO MONTHS LATER

EPILOGUE

Kendall

I stand at the sandy shore of the lake, gazing out at the crystal-clear water, newly melted from its icy state from the past winter; the trees reflect beautifully off of it. Another moment when I can say that I believe everything is perfect. It has been two months since I escaped from the hospital, and I am now in Canada. It took me a minute to find my place in the world without a job at the ready, but I found it, and for the first time I can remember, my mind is still.

My parents were sentenced to life in solitary confinement and were treated as mob bosses in court. Detective Danielle Toole also shared my account of their abuse, which was the nail in the coffin for my parents. The majority of my siblings, with the exception of the ones that were not with Ma'am and Sir at the stadium, were apprehended by the police. Some are going to prison, and some are in foster homes. I don't think I ever loved any of them, but it's a small relief to know they aren't experiencing the full brunt of the Clan. Even more of a relief is the fact that without the Coopers in the picture, the Mors Clan has been severely crippled. It was all over the news, as well as the story of my escape. I guess, in a way, I did get revenge on my parents. Yes, right now, everything is perfect.

I take the letter out of my pocket and feel the paper with my hand before opening it. Writing has never been one of my strong suits, so I read it over five times to make sure it's perfect.

Dear Nat,

Hey. I know we haven't talked in a while, but when we ended
our last conversation, it was kind of abrupt, so I just thought you
might want to know how I've been. When you died, I'm not going
to lie to you, it was hard. You were the most important person in
the world to me, and just like that, you were gone. I know now
that the things I did after that, you would have never wanted
me to do. I was so blinded by rage and grief, I didn't even think
about what you might have wanted for me. So, now that Ma'am
and Sir are no longer a problem, I've been trying to think about
that. What you would have wanted. I'm never going to get over
you, Nat. I couldn't. I know that now. But I guess if I'm always
thinking about you, if I'm always trying to avenge you, you can't
really rest in peace. So what I guess I'm telling you is that I'm
going to stop now. I'm going to stop the killing and robbing and
all that. I'm not going to lie to you, I did bad things and ruined
a lot of lives. But I don't want you to have to worry about me. I
know what you wanted.A life. So I'm trying to stop surviving and
start living. I hope it's enough for the both of us. Day after day,
when I have to make a choice, I think about what you would have
done. It hasn't been easy, but it gets better when I remember it's
for you. Cecelia told me once that in Mexico sometimes people
would write letters to the dead and burn them, or keep them in a
special box to ensure it would reach them. But then, I found this
spot in the woods. It has trees with snow melting off of them,
a lake so clear you can see the Big Dipper off of the reflection.
Somehow, this place just feels like you. I'm sixteen now. I live in

Canada. I don't know where I'm going to go from here. All I know is that I'm going to try to be better. For you.

Love,

   Kendall

   I set the letter in the lake and watch it float out to the middle, slowly becoming more and more transparent until I can't even see it anymore. I look at Natalie's place one more time.

   "I promise I'll try, Nat," I say before I turn around and walk away.

CPSIA information can be obtained
at www.ICGtesting.com
Printed in the USA
LVHW021221070423
743749LV00008B/394